William and the Space Animal

Also published by Macm

* A hardback edition of this title is available from Firecrest Publishing Ltd, Bath, Avon

A STRANGE SIGHT MET THEIR EYES . . . MR REDDITCH
WAS OPENING DRAWERS AND STREWING THEIR CONTENTS
ON THE FLOOR (*see page 68*)

William and the Space Animal

RICHMAL CROMPTON

Illustrated by Thomas Henry

MACMILLAN CHILDREN'S BOOKS

For my great-nephew
EDWARD ASHBEE

First published 1956

Copyright Richmal C. Ashbee

Illustrations copyright Thomas Henry Estate 1956

First published in this edition 1991 by

MACMILLAN CHILDREN'S BOOKS
A division of Macmillan Publishers Limited
London and Basingstoke
Associated companies throughout the world

ISBN 0-333-55546-5

A CIP catalogue record for this book is available from
the British Library

Typeset by Macmillan Production Limited

Printed and bound in Great Britain by
Richard Clay Limited, Bungay, Suffolk

Contents

An invitation from William

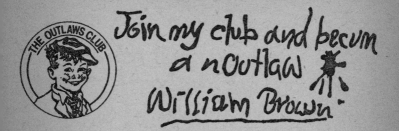

Join my club and becum a n Outlaw
William Brown

You can join the Outlaws Club!
You will receive
� a special Outlaws wallet containing
your own Outlaws badge
the Club Rules
and
a letter from William giving you the secret password

To join the Club send a letter with your name and address written in block capitals telling us you want to join the Outlaws, and a postal order for 45p, to

The Outlaws Club
Children's Marketing Department
18–21 Cavaye Place
London SW10 9PG

You must live in the United Kingdom or the Republic of Ireland in order to join.

Chapter 1

William and the Space Animal

'I think those Spacemen look jolly dull in all the pictures I've seen of them,' said William, 'all covered up like tanks or washing-machines so you can't see their faces prop'ly. It's a Space animal I want to see.'

'Gosh, yes!' said Ginger. 'Space animals ... Yes, I bet they'd be jolly int'restin'. Wonder what they look like.'

'P'raps they're a mixture of every sort of animal there is,' said William.

Ginger turned to look at Jumble, who was burrowing in the ditch, his fox-terrier ears cocked, his spaniel nose quivering, his ragged collie tail waving wildly.

'*He*'d make a good Space animal,' he said.

'Yes, he's a jolly good mixture, is Jumble,' said William, surveying his pet proudly, 'but you can see he's meant to be a *dog*. I bet with a Space animal you wouldn't know what it was meant to be. Gosh! I wish we could find one.'

'P'raps Henry'll know somethin' about them,' said Ginger. The two were on their way to the old barn where they were to meet Henry and Douglas and plan the afternoon's activities. 'Henry gen'rally knows somethin' about everythin'.'

They strolled on down the road, enjoying the sunshine and the feeling of pleasant anticipation that a half-holiday brings with it, a glorious vacuum to be filled by fate with endless opportunities for adventure – opportunities of which the Outlaws seldom failed to take advantage. Having reached the window of the sweet shop, they stopped and examined the wares with frowning concentration.

'Creamy Whirls . . . ' said William. 'They don't look bad.'

'They don't last any time,' said Ginger.

Two women and a man stood near them talking, and the conversations interwove themselves in an inconsequent fashion, neither group taking any notice of the other.

'We're on our way to Aunt Phoebe's birthday party. She's ninety so we simply must put in an appearance.'

'Barley Sugar Fishes . . . Look more like tadpoles to me.'

'I've got Peter off to sleep in his cot and Billy's gone to Micky Fellows' fancy dress party, so everything should be all right.'

'Candy Kisses . . . I wouldn't buy anythin' with a name like that, whatever it tasted like.'

'It's an Alice in Wonderland party and he's gone as the Gryphon.'

'Sherbert . . . That doesn't last any time either.'

'A friend lent us the costume and it's a bit big, but I wedged the head with paper to keep it steady and he *did* look rather sweet.'

'Mixed Fruit Drops . . . We had those last time.'

'It's such a nuisance that it's Flossie's afternoon out – she's our maid, you know – but Mrs Bruster's Milly is coming to baby-sit for us. She's only fourteen but so capable and sensible.'

'Orange Balls . . . Jelly Babies . . . Kid's stuff, Jelly Babies are.'

'Come along, darling. We mustn't miss the bus. Aunt Phoebe will be furious if we aren't there on time.'

'Giant Humbugs.'

'I feel a bit worried about having to come away before Milly actually arrives, but—'

'Yes, you can't go wrong with Giant Humbugs.'

'Flossie will hold the fort till she arrives, dear. Now come along.'

The group dispersed, leaving William and Ginger still weighing up the rival merits of the sweet shop's wares.

'How much money have you got?' said William at last.

'Twopence halfpenny and three farthings,' said Ginger. 'How much have you?'

'Threepence halfpenny an' a farthing. Gosh! That's seven-pence. What'll we buy besides Giant Humbugs?'

'Let's try Golden Nuggets.'

'No . . . Chocolate Buttons. They've got diff'rent tastes inside.'

'No, they're too small.'

'All right. Let's toss for it.'

'All right.'

'Which penny shall we use?'

They considered their store carefully.

'Let's use this one,' said William. 'It looks as if it had a good sort of balance. I'll spin and you call . . . Ready?'

'Heads!' shouted Ginger.

The penny soared through the air at a rakish angle, descended in the gutter and rolled down a grating with a distant 'plop!'

'Well, now *that's* gone,' said Ginger. 'You're a rotten spinner.'

'I'm not,' said William heatedly. 'Its balance wasn't right. I bet it was made by one of those coiners that get sent to prison.' He knelt down and, thrusting Jumble's inquisitive nose aside, peered through the bars of the grate into the murky depth below. 'If I could get it out I'd take it to the p'lice.'

'If we could get it out we could spend it,' said Ginger simply.

William gave a tug at the bars, then abandoned the attempt. Jumble remained there, gazing down through the bars, ears cocked, head on one side, uttering puzzled little growls.

'Well, we've still got sixpence,' said Ginger. 'What'll we buy?'

'Giant Humbugs an' Golden Nuggets. Some of the Chocolate Buttons are goin' mouldy an' I bet those are the ones he'd pick out for us.'

'All right.'

They entered the shop and asked for Giant Humbugs and Golden Nuggets . . . changed their minds when the Golden Nuggets were on the scales and asked for Lime Lollies . . . changed their minds when the Lime Lollies were on the scales and asked for Treacle Dabs . . . and were summarily ejected by the exasperated shopkeeper while in the act of changing their minds yet again and demanding Pineapple Appetisers.

They stopped outside the shop to examine their purchases. Jumble, attracted by the rustling of the paper packets, left his grating and leaped up at them excitedly, eager to claim his share.

'What did we get in the end?' said Ginger, who was in a justifiable state of confusion.

'Giant Humbugs an' Treacle Dabs,' said William. He examined the Treacle Dabs suspiciously. 'I don't b'lieve there's a whole two ounces here.'

'It went down,' said Ginger.

'I bet he's usin' false weights,' said William. 'I—'

Suddenly they saw Frankie Parker coming down the road. He took a paper packet from his pocket as he approached them, selected a sweet and popped it into his mouth.

'Hello,' he said. 'What have you been buying?'

'Giant Humbugs an' Treacle Dabs.'

'I got some Almond Titbits over at Marleigh,' said Frankie. 'They're jolly good. Why don't you go and buy some?'

'We've spent all our money,' said William.

Frankie brought another packet out of his pocket.

'I got some Nougat Squares, too,' he said. 'They're smashing.'

William and Ginger looked wistfully at the colourful slabs.

'Gosh! They look smashing,' agreed William.

'I'll do a swap,' said Frankie in a brisk business-like voice. 'I'll swap a Nougat Square for two of your Treacle Dabs, 'cause they're smaller, aren't they? an' . . . '

Frankie was an expert swapper. He conducted negotiations with swiftness and finesse, and, when finally he set off again down the road, he left William and Ginger gazing thoughtfully at their diminished hoard.

'We don't seem to've got as much as what we started with,' said William.

Ginger's eyes had strayed to the shop window again.

'Gosh, William! Look! We never noticed them. Over in that corner. Liquorice pipes! Gosh! I wish we hadn't spent all that money.'

'Let's see if we can swap something for them,' said William, fired to emulation of Frankie's exploit. 'Come on in.'

The shopkeeper looked up at the clang of the bell and eyed the two customers suspiciously.

'Thought I'd got rid of you two,' he said.

'Well, listen,' said William breathlessly, opening his sticky paper packet. 'We want to swap two Almond Titbits an' a Nougat Square for two liquorice pipes. They come from Marleigh an' they're more int'restin' than anythin' you've got in your shop so you ought to be jolly grateful an'—'

He stopped. The shopkeeper was opening the flap of his counter and once again William and Ginger beat a hasty retreat to the road.

'Gosh, isn't he bad-tempered!' said William. 'He's one of those British trades-people my father was talkin' about las' night. They've got no imagination. They jus' say "Take it or leave it". They don't study the customer.'

'Well, let's start on the Giant Humbugs,' said Ginger. 'They'll last nearly till we've got to the old barn.'

They walked in comparative silence down the road, so much engrossed in the manipulation of the Giant Humbugs that at first they did not notice the woman who was signalling to them from a small cottage.

'You goin' through the village?' she said when at last they saw her signals and stopped at the door.

'Yeh,' said William indistinctly.

'Well, will you call at The Hawthorns and leave a message for me?'

There was a pause during which William tried to manoeuvre his Giant Humbug into a better position. Failing, he uttered a snort that signified assent.

'Well, tell 'em I'm sorry, but our Milly can't come baby-mindin' this afternoon. She's got a cold in 'er 'ead something chronic. Sneezin' fit to fetch the chimneys down, she is.'

William gave the joke the tribute of a guffaw that deposited his Giant Humbug on the whitened doorstep. He picked it up, brushed it on his sleeve and replaced it in his mouth.

'I jus' cleaned that,' said the woman indignantly. 'Now off you go an' give the message same as I told you an' no more of your monkey-tricks!'

'All right, all right,' said William, managing to instil a hint of dignity into his muffled voice. 'C'm on, Ginger.'

The two proceeded down the road in silence for some minutes.

'Mine's gettin' near the end,' said William at last.

'So's mine.'

'I'm goin' to start chewin' now.'

'So'm I.'

They crunched with noisy enjoyment till suddenly Ginger

stopped and pointed to a house. 'The Hawthorns . . . I say! Isn't that the house she gave us a message for? Let's go now an' give it an' get it over. Douglas an' Henry'll be wonderin' what's happened to us. We wasted *hours* in that sweet shop.'

'Yes,' agreed William sombrely. 'He didn't study the customer. He's jus' like the ones my father was talkin' about. He'll never attract overseas trade.'

'Well, come on,' said Ginger, going up to the front door and preparing to ring the bell.

But there was no need to ring the bell. The door flew open at their approach and a taut, trim girl, wearing hat and coat, her thin body a-quiver with impatience, stood on the threshold.

'Better late than never!' she snapped. 'Thought you was never comin'.' She surveyed them, her small sharp nose raised contemptuously. 'Well, I mus' say she's got queer ideas of baby-minders. Kid of a girl, it was, last time. Two kids of boys, this time. Well, it's none of my business an' I'm late enough as it is, so stand out of me way an' I'll be off!'

'Yes, but—' began William as the sinister implication of the words slowly dawned on him.

She interrupted him, thrusting him aside.

'Kid's asleep upstairs,' she said shortly. 'Other kid's out at a fancy dress party, but someone's bringin' it back an' it can put itself to bed, more or less. There's sandwiches on a tray in the kitchen. Television's out of order. Radio's on the bookcase in the sitting-room. An' now it's all yours, so good-bye an' good luck.'

'Yes, but—' began William again.

The girl had hurried down the path to the gate and was running along the road to the bus-stop.

'Hi!' shouted William, running after her. 'Hi! *Listen!*'

He was too late. A bus slowed down, the girl leaped upon it and almost immediately it gained speed and was vanishing into the distance.

'Gosh!' he said 'She's gone!'

'An' left us mindin' the baby,' said Ginger.

William swallowed the last fragment of his Giant Humbug with a gulp.

'Gosh!' he said again, in a voice so charged with emotion that it was little more than a whisper. 'She *can't* have!'

'Well, she has,' said Ginger. 'She said she had. She said, "It's all yours". She meant she'd left us mindin' the baby.'

'Well, what'll we do?' said William.

'Let's jus' take no notice an' go on to the old barn.'

'No, we can't do that,' said William slowly. Hidden deep beneath the lawlessness of William's composition was a sense of responsibility – erratic and unreliable and functioning only intermittently, but still, in its fashion, a sense of responsibility – and occasionally it surprised even William by asserting itself in a crisis. 'We can't jus' go off an' do that. We can't jus' leave it . . . Well, let's go in an' have a look, anyway.'

They returned to the house and entered by the front door that Flossie had left open. They looked into a pleasant sitting-room and went through to the kitchen where they found a tray of sandwiches and biscuits on the table. In silence and by tacit consent they divided these and disposed of them in a few capacious mouthfuls. Jumble found a rubbish pail beneath the sink and, overturning it with a skill born of long practice, set to work on some bacon rinds and a couple of cold potatoes.

Then they went into the sitting-room and turned on the radio.

'The Devonian fauna is intermediate in character between the Silurian and the Carboniferous . . . ' a cultured, resonant voice informed them.

They turned off the radio and went out of the sitting-room.

'She said it was upstairs,' said William, standing uncertainly at the foot of the staircase. 'We'd better go an' have a look at it.'

Slowly and a little apprehensively, they climbed the stair-case and entered the front bedroom.

In a cot against the wall, a rosy curly-haired baby lay sleeping beneath a pale blue coverlet heavily bedecked with white rabbits.

William stood, gazing down at it.

'Looks quite a sensible one,' he said critically. 'It isn't yelling, anyway.'

'It might start any minute,' said Ginger nervously. 'Come on. Let's leave it. It's all right. Let's go to the old barn an' leave it.'

'No, we can't do that,' said William again. 'There's lors against leavin' babies alone in houses. They get kidnapped.' His drooping spirits rose. 'Gosh! It'd be smashin' if a kidnapper came to try. I bet we could fix him all right. We could start throwin' things at him before he got to the top of the stairs. I could throw water down on him out of the bathroom. I could hurl boulders down on him if I could find any. I've always wanted to hurl boulders down on someone.' He opened a cupboard and looked into it. 'There's a suit-case here that'd make a jolly good boulder.'

Ginger stood at the window gazing disconsolately up and down the empty road.

'Well, there aren't even any kidnappers comin',' he said. 'How long have we got to stay like this?'

William closed the cupboard.

'Till someone comes back,' he said

'It's goin' to be an awful waste of time,' grumbled Ginger. 'Jus' lookin' at a baby for hours an' *hours*. It's enough to drive anyone ravin' mad.'

'We could do it in turns,' said William thoughtfully. 'You could go to Henry an' Douglas at the old barn an' then come back an' then I could go an' then come back.'

'*That's* not goin' to be much fun,' said Ginger.

'No, it isn't,' agreed William. He looked at the baby and a light broke suddenly over his frowning countenance. 'I *say*! I've got an idea.'

'What?'

'We could take it with us.'

'Gosh!' It was Ginger's turn to feel the stirrings of conscience. 'We can't do that, William.'

'Why not?' said William. 'We'd be mindin' it, wouldn't we? I don't see it makes any diff'rence whether we mind it here or in the old barn. Come to that' – as usual, once William had conceived an idea, arguments in favour of it flocked into his mind – 'I think we *ought* to take it to the old barn. It'd get some fresh air if we took it to the old barn an' it's not gettin' any here.'

'The windows are open,' Ginger pointed out.

'Yes, but there isn't any wind blowin' fresh air through them. I bet this air's been here all day an' it mus' be jolly bad for the baby bein' in old air like this. I bet that's what real baby-minders do – take 'em out an' give em' a bit of fresh air – an' I bet its mother'll be jolly grateful to us for takin' it out an' givin' it a bit of fresh air. Stands to reason she will.'

Ginger tried to find a flaw in this argument, then gave up the attempt and set himself to the discussion of ways and means.

'How're you goin' to get it there?' he said. He examined the cot. 'P'raps we could carry this bed thing between us. It doesn't look very heavy.'

'No, we'll jus' carry the baby,' said William. 'It's easy enough carryin' babies. I carried one of my aunt's once an' I didn't drop it. I nearly did but I caught it again. It's not like carryin' square things like boxes. They go into any sort of shape, babies do. They're jolly easy to carry.'

'We'll have to take somethin' to keep it warm,' said Ginger, eyeing the occupant of the cot with increased misgiving.

'I know they've got to be kept warm. They've got to be made into sort of *parcels* with warm stuff. I've seen 'em out in prams.'

'Oh, we'll manage that all right,' said William. He spoke airily, but something of his confidence ebbed as he looked down at his sleeping cargo. 'We've got to pick it up first of all.'

'How'll we do that?' said Ginger. 'Will you take its head an' me its feet?'

'No, I'll do it,' said William. His face was set and strained with resolve. 'I'll do it. I'll count one . . . two . . . three . . . and then I'll do it.' He drew a deep breath. 'One . . . two . . . three . . .'

'Go!' said Ginger.

Making a desperate lunge, William dived into the cot and emerged with the baby. The baby opened blue eyes, gurgled contentedly, then nestled back against William's shoulder.

'Seems to like me,' said William with a bashful smile.

'Well, let's get it packed up,' said Ginger, taking an armful of blankets from the cot.

The baby showed surprising co-operation and docility, allowing blankets to be wrapped and poked and swathed about it with only an occasional grunt, settling back to sleep again finally in William's arms. He was evidently a philo-sophic baby with a knack of accommodating himself to cir-cumstances.

'Well, now, come on,' said William, stepping carefully down the stairs with his burden.

Jumble, having completed his investigation of the rubbish pail, had joined them in the hall, leaping up to examine the new addition to the party.

'I don't know that we're doin' right, William,' said Ginger thoughtfully.

''Course we are,' said William, combating his own secret

doubts. 'We're givin' it fresh air. Gosh! I dunno what would have happened to it if we'd left it in that room with all that old air. It might have died of some disease.'

'Oh, well,' said Ginger, as usual resigning himself in advance to whatever complications the adventure might bring with it, 'I don't expect we could get it back in that bed like it was before now even if we tried, so we might as well go on with it. Shall we leave the front door closed or open?'

'Closed,' said William, adding virtuously, 'We've got to look after the house prop'ly as well as mind the baby. We're doin' it jolly well, so far, I think. I don't see why they shouldn't pay us a lot of money when they come back.'

'I bet they won't,' said Ginger.

'Have a dig in my pocket for Frankie's Almond Titbits,' said William. 'This baby takes both my arms. Gosh! It's heavier than you'd think.'

The baby had accommodated itself to William's vice-like clutch and was sleeping peacefully.

They walked along the road, munching Almond Titbits and gazing with awed interest at their sleeping burden. There were few passers-by and such as passed paid scant attention to the sight of a small boy, carrying, presumably, an infant brother or sister.

Henry and Douglas were standing at the door of the old barn.

Their mouths dropped open in amazement as they saw the trio approaching.

'What on earth have you brought that for?' said Henry.

'We're mindin' it,' said William, 'an' we've brought it along for a bit of fresh air.' He hastened to forestall criticism by adopting a tone of amused superiority. 'Haven't you ever heard of givin' babies a bit of fresh air? Gosh! You mus' be ign'rant.'

'Yes, but what are we goin' to *do* with it?' demanded Henry.

'WE'VE BROUGHT IT ALONG FOR A BIT OF FRESH AIR,'
SAID WILLIAM.

'We'll look after it in turn,' said William. His eye wandered round the barn and came to rest on Douglas, who stood in the background, gazing in a fascinated manner at the baby, his mouth still hanging open. 'Douglas can start.'

'No!' protested Douglas. 'I don't know anythin' about them. I—'

'You needn't,' said William. 'This one is all right. It jus' goes on sleepin' . . . We'll share any money Ginger an' me get for mindin' it so you all ought to be jolly glad to help. Sit down on that box.' He pushed the feebly protesting Douglas down on to the ramshackle packing-case and thrust the baby at him, arranging Douglas's arms and the baby's blankets with a ferocious scowl and an almost maternal precision. 'Keep it jus' like that an' it'll go on sleepin'. It does . . . ' He dived into his pocket, brought out the sticky paper packet of sweets, carefully selecting a Nougat Square and a Treacle Dab and laying them on the ground by Douglas's feet. 'You can be eatin' those an' we'll go out now an' we'll come back in turns to mind the baby.'

'Yes, but – *listen!*' wailed Douglas. 'I don't *want* to mind it. I don't know *how* to mind it. I—'

He was wailing to the empty air. William, Ginger, Henry and Jumble were already crossing the field in the direction of the woods.

'How did you get it?' said Henry in an aggrieved tone.

'Oh, never mind that ole baby,' said William carelessly. The problem of the baby had been solved, as he considered, to the satisfaction of everyone concerned and he dismissed it from his mind. 'What'll we do now?'

'Gosh! I thought you were never comin',' said Henry, still harping on his grievances. 'I was late myself 'cause of this aunt, but – well, I began to think that somethin' had happened to you.'

'Well, it had,' said William. 'What aunt?'

'An' ole aunt that came to lunch an' stayed talkin' an' talkin'.'

'What about?' said William, who took an ever-fresh interest in his neighbours and their concerns. 'What was she like an' what did she talk about?'

'She was awful an' she talked about the power of thought,' said Henry gloomily. 'She b'lieves you can make things happen by thinkin' about 'em.'

William gave this a moment's frowning consideration.

'Well, you can't,' he said.

'She says you can. She'd been to a lecture by a man that

knew. He'd been out to the East an' met Eastern people that *did* it. One of them lay on nails an' didn't feel it 'cause of this power of thought.'

'Well, I don't see any sense in lyin' on nails, anyway,' said Ginger. 'I'd as soon not do it as do it.'

'Yes, but they did *other* things. They jus' *thought* things an' they happened.'

'They mus' think jolly hard to make them axshully *happen*.'

'Well, I 'spect they did.'

'Might be worth tryin',' said William after a pause.

'How d'you mean?'

'This power of thought. Might be worth tryin' to do it.'

'But you don't know how to.'

'I bet I do,' said William. 'Well, if these Eastern people could do it, I bet I could. I'd think harder an' harder an' *harder* for minutes an' minutes an' *minutes* till I'd got this power of thought goin' then I'd wish.'

'What would you wish?' said Henry, impressed by William's earnestness.

William considered.

'I know!' he said at last. 'Ginger an' me were talkin' about it jus' now. I'd wish a Space animal to come. I'm sick of pictures of Spacemen. I want to see a Space animal.'

'I bet you won't. Not with jus' thinkin'.'

'All right. You wait an' see,' said William. 'I'm goin' to start now . . . ' They had entered the wood and the path before them wound through the trees, then swerved sharply out of sight. 'I'm goin' to think hard till we get to that turn, then I'm goin' to wish. Now I'm goin' to start, so shut up.'

Walking on either side of William, Henry and Ginger watched his face with growing concern. It was set and scowling. The power of thought evidently precluded the function of breathing, for it turned pink, then red, then purple . . . the veins on his forehead became congested, his cheeks bulged.

THROUGH THE UNDERGROWTH CAME A SMALL GREEN
FIGURE. 'GOSH!' SAID WILLIAM.

'I say, stop it, William,' said Ginger anxiously. 'You're
goin' to burst.'

William had reached the turn of the path. He stopped, let
out his breath in a prolonged puff and gasped:

'I wish to see a Space animal.'

And then – through the undergrowth between the trees
came a small green figure with green head, green wings,

green body, green tail. It walked disconsolately and wailed as
t walked.

'Gosh!' said William faintly. 'A Space animal!' The purple
colour brought into his face by the process of thought had
faded to an almost ashen hue. 'Gosh! I've *done* it.'

As if attracted by his voice, the creature turned and
approached him. The wails died away to a whimpering.

'Good—' began William reassuringly and ended somewhat
amely, 'Space animal!' as he patted the green head.

Jumble, after a moment's doubt, had evidently decided to
admit the newcomer into his large circle of friends and
acquaintances and was leaping up in welcome, wagging his
ail.

'Seems quite tame,' said William, 'an' Jumble likes it.'

'It's jolly int'restin',' said Ginger, walking round it. 'It's quite diff'rent from any animal we've got on the earth, isn't it?'

'Yes . . . it's got claws an' paws.' said William.

'An' wings.'

'An' ears an' a beak.'

'Funny sort of noise it makes,' said Henry as the wailing began again.

'Bit like a cat,' said Ginger.

'Or a hyena,' said William.

'Or a factory whistle,' said Ginger.

Then Henry asked the pertinent question.

'What are we goin' to do with it?'

'Y-yes,' said William, wrinkling his brows. 'Now we've brought it down from Mars or the Moon or wherever it comes from, we've got to treat it right.'

'We don't know what it eats,' said Ginger.

William brought out his sticky paper packet, carefully selected a Treacle Dab and offered it to the newcomer. The newcomer showed neither pleasure nor interest.

'I'll put it on the ground by it,' said William, placing the Treacle Dab on the ground by the visitor. 'It might be used to eatin' off the ground.'

Still the creature showed neither pleasure nor interest.

'It doesn't like it,' said William, picking up the Treacle Dab and replacing it in the packet.

'Well, we'll have to feed it,' said Ginger. 'We can't let it starve.'

'An' where'll we keep it?' said Henry.

'We could keep it a week in turns,' said William.

'Yes, an' everyone'll find out,' said Ginger. 'You can't keep a Space animal like that secret.'

'Wonder what they think's happened to it up in Mars or the Moon,' said William. 'I s'pose it jus' disappeared.'

'Hope it doesn't start a Space war,' said Ginger, glancing anxiously up at the sky.

The Space animal was sitting on the ground, whimpering a little but obviously taking comfort from their presence.

'Grown-up people that find strange animals give them to the zoo,' said Henry.

'Yes, we could do that,' said William. 'We could give it to the zoo.'

'We don't know how to get it there,' objected Ginger. 'Anyway, we haven't any money to buy its ticket an' I 'spect they'd charge an awful lot of money for it on the railway.'

'There's the British Museum,' said Henry. 'People sometimes give things they find to the British Museum . . . '

'Yes,' said William indignantly, 'an' it'd have a jolly dull time there with statchoos an' mummies an' things. No, it's not goin' to the British Museum.' Suddenly the light of an idea broke through the gloom of his countenance. '*Tell* you what!'

'Yes?' they chorused eagerly.

'We could take it to Emmett's animal shop an' sell it to him. It'd be all right there.'

'He wouldn't buy that insect collection you tried to sell him,' said Ginger.

'Well, he wasn't int'rested in insects,' said William. 'He'd be int'rested in a Space animal. Stands to reason. Anyone'd be int'rested in a Space animal. I bet he'd give us a jolly lot of money for it. An' he'll know what to feed it on an' if the zoo wants it they can come an' get it off him. Let's go there with it now.'

'All right,' agreed the others.

William took a paw of the Space animal in his hand.

'Come on, ole boy,' he said. 'Come on, ole Space animal.'

It grasped his hand trustingly and began to trot along beside him, the whimpers dying away to a murmur.

They went across the fields and along the main street of Hadley. Passers-by threw them amused and curious glances, but no one stopped or questioned them. Having arrived at Emmett's animal shop, they paused to look in at the window . . . puppies, kittens, hamsters, rabbits, guinea-pigs, tortoises, goldfish in bowls, birds in cages . . .

'Look, he's got all sorts,' said William, 'an' they all seem jolly happy. I bet a Space animal'd settle down with 'em all right. He knows what to give 'em to eat an' I bet he'd know what to give a Space animal. He could try diff'rent sorts of animal food on it, anyway. An' it'll look jolly fine in the window there.'

'It's a bit big,' said Ginger, looking down at their exhibit.

'Well, he can keep it in the shop. He can keep it in a dog kennel. I bet he'll sell it for pounds an' *pounds* when people come to know about it. Gosh! It mus' be the only one in England. I bet the zoo'll want it as soon as they hear about it. I bet—'

'Well, come on in,' interrupted Henry, who was beginning to wear a faintly harassed air now that the affair was nearing its crisis.

William opened the shop door and entered, holding his charge by the paw, followed by Henry, Ginger and Jumble.

A vague-looking boy of about thirteen came forward.

'My uncle's jus' gone out,' he said in an adenoidal voice. 'He said if any customers came they was to wait an' he'd be back in a minute.'

'Well, we're in a hurry,' said William importantly. 'We've come to sell a Space animal.'

'A—?' The boy looked down at the small green figure and a spark of interest came into his impassive face. 'A – what did you say?'

'A Space animal,' repeated William impatiently. 'Have you never heard of a Space animal? It's the only one in England an' it's jolly valu'ble. We're chargin' ' – he drew a

'IT'S THE ONLY ONE IN ENGLAND AN' IT'S JOLLY
VALU'BLE,' SAID WILLIAM.

deep breath – 'five pounds for it. I bet it's worth a hundred.'

'Or a thousand,' said Ginger.

'But we'd take less,' put in Henry hastily. 'We'd take ten shillings.'

'Or even five,' said William.

'We wouldn't mind two an' six,' said Ginger.

A loud wail came from the green head.

'That's the noise they make, Space animals,' said William. 'Well, what about it?'

The spark of interest had faded from the boy's impassive face.

'He said I'd not got to sell nothin',' he said. 'He said I was to tell customers he'd be back in a minute.'

'Well, look!' William's eyes had strayed to a shallow box of baby tortoises. 'We'll swap it for a baby tortoise. Gosh! Your uncle'll be jolly glad to find you've swapped a baby tortoise for a valu'ble Space animal. That's a *bargain*, that is.'

'I dunno . . . ' said the boy doubtfully.

'He'll be *mad* with you if he comes back an' finds you've let a bargain like that go . . . a valu'ble Space animal for jus' a baby tortoise. If you'll let me have the baby tortoise you can have the Space animal now at once an' you'll prob'ly have made your fortune. You'll be *famous*. You'll have your picture in the *newspapers*. It's the only Space animal in the whole world, I tell you, an'—'

'Oh, all right,' said the boy, overwhelmed by the torrent of William's eloquence.

'Thanks,' said William.

He carefully selected a baby tortoise and slipped it into his pocket.

'There you are!' he said, giving the Space animal a gentle push towards its new owner.

At that moment the shop door opened and Mr Emmett appeared.

He eyed the customers without enthusiasm.

'What's all this?' he said.

'We've come to sell a Space animal,' said William. 'It's worth hundreds of pounds but we'll take five.'

'Or ten shillings,' said Henry.

'Or two an' six,' said Ginger.

Another wail rose from the green head.

'That's the noise they make,' explained William again.

Mr Emmett strode across the shop, took hold of the green head and wrenched it off, revealing a round rosy face, scratched and tear-stained, which broke into a beam of delight when disclosed to view.

'I was a Gryphon an' I got stuck,' explained the Space animal. 'I got stuck in my head so it hurt me an' I couldn't see anything so I ran away an' I cried but it's all right now.'

'Gosh!' gasped William. 'It's not one, after all.'

Mr Emmett's grim features did not relax.

'Clear out, the lot of you!' he said. 'Any more of your nonsense and—'

But already William was leading his band in disordered flight into the street. Jumble, who had stayed to secure a dog biscuit from an overflowing sack, brought up the rear. In the street they stopped and looked at each other. The small boy's face was still wreathed in smiles. He had picked up his head and was carrying it under his arm.

'I was stuck in it,' he explained again. 'He unstuck me. He was a kind man.'

'Well, you can go home now,' said William coldly. 'We've taken a lot of trouble over you all for nothing.'

'Can't go home,' said the child, with another engaging smile. 'Lost.'

'Well, you've been enough of a nuisance already,' said William sternly. He felt a natural resentment against the erstwhile Space animal. 'You've wasted hours an' *hours* of our time an' you can jolly well go away now.'

The boy beamed at him.

'I got stuck in it,' he said, evidently considering that his adventure had not been accorded its due meed of interest. 'I was a Gryphon an' I got stuck in it.'

'Oh, come on,' said William, turning to the others with an air of disgust.

They set off again across the fields. The small boy accompanied them, his face still wearing its all-embracing smile. Jumble trotted at his heels, every now and then leaping up at the Gryphon's head. Each time he did it, the small boy's laugh pealed out.

'Dog likes it,' he said delightedly. 'Look! Dog likes it.'

When they reached the wood the three Outlaws sat down beneath a tree to consider the situation. The small boy sat with them, still chuckling at Jumble's attempts to investigate the head.

'What's your name?' said William sternly.

The boy thought for a minute.

'Gryphon,' he said at last proudly.

'Do you live near here?'

'Yes.'

'Were you going home when we found you?'

'Yes.'

'Can't you say anything but "yes"?'

'Yes.'

'Well, say it,'

'Yes.'

Freed of the encumbrance of his head, he was a frolicsome child with a pronounced if crude sense of humour.

'Ask me some more,' he shouted. 'Ask me some more an' I'll say "yes".'

His merriment was infectious.

'You're an idiot, aren't you?' said Ginger.

'Yes,' chuckled the child.

'Do you have frog pie for tea?' said Henry.

'Yes.'

'Do you go to bed in the chimney?'

'Yes.'

The four of them rolled about in mirth. The small boy, shouting with delight, turned a somersault backwards. Jumble took it as an invitation to a game of the rougher variety and sprang upon him, tearing with playful ferocity at the green suit in which he was enveloped. The boy's laughter and Jumble's mock growls rang out as piece after piece of the flimsy costume gave way before Jumble's onslaught. Feathers flew in all directions as he tore off the wings . . . lengths of material and cardboard strewed the ground. He worried them and tossed them into the air, taking the laughter and applause as encouragement to further effort. Finally he set to work on the head, which had rolled to the foot of the tree, chewing, worrying, growling.

The small boy stood up, still chuckling with delight, but the delight of the Outlaws faded somewhat as they surveyed him. The Gryphon suit was now a mere frill round his plump waist. The upper part hung precariously from his shoulders.

'Gosh!' said William. 'What are you goin' to do now? Are you goin' home?'

'Yes,' said the boy, turning to set off among the trees.

'Do you know the way?' said William.

The boy's voice came from the distance, high-pitched with laughter.

'Yes,' it said.

'He wasn't a bad kid,' said Ginger, 'an' a real Space animal might have been a bit of a nuisance. I 'spect this power of thought gets a bit muddled. I mean, you wished for a Space animal an' it got you the nearest it could find. I mean, it got you somethin' that *looked* like a Space animal.'

But William wasn't listening. A dreamy expression had come into his face.

'Gosh!' he said. 'I've jus' remembered somethin'.'

'What?'

'That baby we're s'posed to be mindin'.' He stood up. 'We'd better be gettin' back to it.'

'It'll be all right,' Ginger reassured him. 'Douglas is with it.'

'Yes, but we said we'd go an' take our turns. He'll be gettin' mad with us. Come on.'

They set off briskly towards the old barn. It lay silent and peaceful in the sunshine.

'It's not started yelling yet, anyway,' said Henry. 'I knew ole Douglas'd manage all right.'

They reached the open doorway and looked into the dim recesses of the barn.

Douglas was there, turning over a heap of old sacks in the farther corner, his face wearing an expression of tense anxiety.

'Where's the baby?' said William.

'I don't know,' said Douglas. 'It's gone.'

'Gone!' echoed William. 'It couldn't have. It can't walk.'

'Well, it has,' said Douglas. 'You went on and on not comin' an' I couldn't think what'd happened to you an' I thought I'd jus' go as far as the end of the wood an' see if I could see you an' it seemed all right 'cause it was still asleep so I put it down on these sacks an' went to try'n find you an' I couldn't so I came back an' – it'd gone.' He continued to turn over the sacks with a distracted air. 'It isn't anywhere here at all. I've looked everywhere.'

'Gosh! *Now* you've done it!' said William, aghast.

'Losin' a baby! There's lors against it. I bet we'll all get put in prison.'

'But it couldn't walk,' protested Douglas.

'It may've started to walk while you were out. They *do* start to walk. It may've come over it quite sudden how to walk while you were out.'

'It may have crawled,' said Ginger. 'I've seen them crawling.'

'Well, anyway,' said William, 'let's go'n' have a good look

through the woods 'case it's there. Gosh! Its mother'll be in an awful state.'

Its mother was not in an awful state. She was walking with her husband from the station discussing Aunt Phoebe's party in a placid leisurely fashion.

'She's a dear old thing,' she said, 'and she was so glad to see us.'

'Yes,' agreed her husband. 'It was quite worth making the effort to go.'

'It was lucky we could get Milly to mind Peter and lucky that Billy was going to the party. He did look sweet in his Gryphon suit, didn't he?'

Mr Clayton smiled.

'He looked the young ruffian he is,' he said.

'It'll be lovely to get home again and find Peter asleep in his cot and—'

'Mrs Clayton!' called a voice behind them.

They turned to see Miss Milton hurrying along the road, her small face pursed in anxiety.

They stopped.

'What's the matter, Miss Milton?'

'Oh dear!' panted Miss Milton. 'Oh dear! I'm in such a state I hardly know what to do. I've just found an abandoned baby in that old barn in the field.'

'An—?'

'An abandoned baby. I've been over to see some friends at Marleigh and I was coming home by the short cut across the fields and I just glanced in at the door of the barn and there I saw it – an abandoned baby.'

'What did you do?' said Mrs Clayton.

'I picked it up and took it home,' said Miss Milton. 'I couldn't think of anything else to do. I couldn't leave it there abandoned to die of exposure, though it *had* a lot of blankets with it. Anyway, I brought it home and now I'm on my way to tell the police about it, but I'm feeling terribly worried because I've no one to leave it with and I've left it alone in the house tucked up on the settee and though it looks quite comfortable *anything* might happen to it.'

'Why don't you bring it to our house?' said Mrs Clayton. 'Go and fetch it and we'll look after it while you go to the police.' She smiled. 'We've got one baby, you know, and another wouldn't make much difference.'

'Oh, thank you so much,' said Miss Milton. 'What a good idea! That's a great relief. I'll fetch it now.'

She turned and scuttled off down the road.

'What an extraordinary thing!' said Mr Clayton. 'Whoever would abandon a baby in a barn?'

'People do,' said Mrs Clayton. 'You read about it in newspapers . . . Well, the darling can share Peter's things till some arrangement has been made for him. He—' She stopped short. Another figure had appeared, hurrying – almost running – down the road towards them. 'Whoever's this? Why, it's Mrs Monks.'

Mrs Monks came up to them. Her face, like Miss Milton's, was pursed in anxiety.

'Oh, dear!' she said. 'I should so like your advice. I've just found a little lost boy.'

'A little—?'

'A little lost boy. I think he's one of that family of Hungarian acrobats who were performing at the circus at Hadley last week. They went this morning and must have left the child behind in the confusion. I didn't see them myself but I heard that they all wore little green frills and that's what he's wearing and the youngest was about four years old and he seems about that age. I asked him his name and he said something that sounded like Gaifon. A Hungarian name undoubtedly. I asked him if he was Hungarian and he said "Yes". I asked him if he was one of the family of acrobats and he said "Yes". I asked him if he was lost and he said "Yes". He seemed to understand English but not speak it much. Quite a cheerful little boy . . . but I must of course try to get into touch with his parents at once.'

'Where is he now?' said Mrs Clayton.

'That's what's worrying me. I took him home and made him some bread and milk and then I thought I'd go and tell the police. So much more satisfactory to do these things personally . . . Besides, I can never hear what that man at the police-station says on the telephone. He has a most indistinct voice. But I *am* a bit worried about leaving the child alone in the house. I didn't want to take him through the village in his acrobat costume and yet it's just struck me that he might possibly wander out of the house and get lost again . . . I really don't know what to do.'

'Run back home and bring him along to our house,' said Mrs Clayton. 'We're going to have an extra baby anyway, so an extra little boy won't make any difference. We'll keep him happy and comfortable till they've made some arrangement about sending him on to the circus.' She turned to her husband with a smile. '*Four* children now, darling, but I think we can cope.'

'Sure!' said Mr Clayton.

He was the sort of man who takes things in his stride.

'Oh, that's splendid,' said Mrs Monks. 'I'll run back now and fetch him to you then I'll go and make my personal report to the police.'

She hurried back down the road and Mrs and Mr Clayton strolled on towards their house.

'I shall have to get busy with blankets and things for our two little visitors,' said Mrs Clayton. 'Fortunately I've got heaps. Mother was so deliciously Victorian in stocking us up with *dozens* of everything.'

'Well, there's something in it,' said Mr Clayton.

He unlocked the door, and they entered the hall.

'Milly!' called Mrs Clayton in a pleasant tone of greeting.

There was no answer.

'Milly!' called Mrs Clayton, a note of anxiety replacing the pleasant note of greeting.

There was no answer.

'Milly!' she called again, a note of anguish replacing the anxiety.

'Milly!' called Mr Clayton with a mixture of foreboding, bewilderment and male authority.

There was no answer.

Mrs Clayton ran upstairs to the bedroom and stood for a few moments, paralysed by horror, gazing down at the empty cot.

'He's gone,' she screamed. 'Peter's gone!'

Mr Clayton took the stairs three at a time and gazed aghast at the disordered sheets and coverlet.

'What on earth's happened?' he said.

'He's been kidnapped,' wailed Mrs Clayton. 'They've taken him, blankets and all. They've *kidnapped* him.' She went into the next room and gave another scream. 'Billy's not here either. He should have been back from the party long ago.'

'Where's Milly?' said Mr Clayton.

'They've murdered her and kidnapped the two children,' said Mrs Clayton hysterically.

Mr Clayton conducted a hasty search of the house.

'There's no trace of any of them,' he said.

At that moment came a knocking at the door, and Mrs Clayton went down to open it.

Mrs Fellowes stood there.

'I hope Billy got home all right,' she said.

'He's not here,' said Mrs Clayton wildly. 'He's been kidnapped.'

'Kidnapped?'

'When did he leave your party?' said Mr Clayton.

'Some time ago,' said Mrs Fellowes. 'His Gryphon head got jammed and he went home. At least so the other children told me. I meant to ring you up but, what with all the uproar and little Susie Parker being sick and little Ella Poppleham cutting her head open on the fireguard and Maisie falling downstairs, I haven't had a second even to *think* till now and then I thought I might as well come round and make sure it was all right.'

'It isn't,' said Mrs Clayton, her face stony with despair. 'They've all gone. They've been murdered and kidnapped, all of them.'

'I'm going to the police-station now,' said Mr Clayton, 'and then I'm going to scour the countryside.'

They went down to the gate and there they stopped. Two women were approaching from opposite directions. One carried a baby, the other led a small boy wearing what looked like a tattered green tunic.

'Oh, dear!' said Mrs Clayton, 'Those two children we said we'd take in – the abandoned baby and the little acrobat. We must tell them we can't have them now. Quick, dear! I'll tell Miss Milton and you tell Mrs Monks. There isn't a minute to spare.'

She ran down the road to Miss Milton.

'I'm so sorry, Miss Milton,' she said, 'A dreadful thing has happened. I'm afraid we can't take—' She stopped and looked down at the face of the sleeping baby. '*Peter!*' she screamed.

Mr Clayton had approached Mrs Monks.

'I'm very sorry, Mrs Monks,' he said, 'but I'm afraid it will be impossible for us to—' He looked down at the small face upraised to his in a beaming smile and gave a yell of delight. '*Billy!*' he shouted.

* * *

Dusk was falling as William walked down the road. Ginger, sent on a reconnoitring expedition, had reported the course of events. One small child had seen the Outlaws entering the wood with Billy in his Gryphon suit, another had seen William and Ginger carrying the baby to the barn, and both had duly reported these facts. The net was closing round the Outlaws and they knew that retribution awaited them at home. William's steps were slow and dragging. He had put off the moment of return as long as possible, but it could be put off no longer.

Plunging his hands into his pockets with a despondent gesture he was surprised to find one of them in contact with a hard shell. The baby tortoise! He had forgotten the baby tortoise . . . He took it out and held it on his palm. It poked its head from its shell and looked round in an inquiring fashion. The gloom cleared from his countenance.

'I'll swap you a Treacle Dab for it,' said a voice and he looked up to find Frankie Parker standing before him, gazing enviously at the tortoise.

'No,' said William.

'Two Treacle Dabs.'

'No. I won't swap it at all.'

'How did you get it?' said Frankie irritably. 'You said you hadn't any money.'

William was silent for a moment as his mind went over the events of the day, already blurred and confused by the passage of time. He straightened his drooping shoulders. Something of dignity invested his bedraggled figure.

'I got it,' he said loftily, 'by the power of thought.'

Chapter 2

William Goes for a Nice Little Walk

'Why are you doin' all this muddlin' about?' said William, throwing an interested glance round the disordered room.

'I'm spring-cleaning, dear,' said Mrs Brown, 'and get out of the way.'

'But it's not spring,' objected William. 'You can't do spring-cleanin' when it's not spring.'

'I know it's not spring, dear, but I had 'flu in the spring and had to put it off. Now *do* get out of the way.'

'Well, I don't mind helpin' a bit with spring-cleanin',' said William, his interest increasing as he inspected the chaos that surrounded him. 'I did help last year, didn't I?'

'If you call it helping,' said Mrs Brown, plunging the vacuum cleaner attachment into the recesses of the settee. 'You scrubbed your father's chair, loose cover and all, and left it *sodden*. Dripping with water right through to the floor. He was furious. He couldn't use it for weeks.'

'Well, it was clean,' said William after a moment's thought. 'An' I'm a year older than that now. I've got a good bit more sense than I had all that time ago. An' anyway it was a *sens'ble* thing to do. That water goin' right through cleaned the inside. I bet you'd've only cleaned the outside, your way. I bet that chair's never been so clean in its life as what it was when I'd finished with it.'

'Even after it was dry it gave your father lumbago . . . Do leave the vacuum alone, William.'

'I was only wonderin' how it worked . . . Well, what can I do to help?'

'You can go away,' said Mrs Brown. 'You can go for a nice little walk.'

'Oh, all right,' said William distantly, 'if you don't *want* me to help . . . but I bet I *could* help all right.'

There was a look of purpose on his face as he went from the room that might have raised doubts in Mrs Brown's mind had it not been wholly given to the curious assortment of oddments – hairpins, crumbs, pencils and even a pair of scissors – that had lodged between the arm and seat of the settee . . . Peace seemed to descend on the house, broken only by the humming of the vacuum cleaner. He's gone for a nice little walk, thought Mrs Brown happily, as she started on the other side of the settee. One wonders where all the dirt comes from . . . I'll get the carpets out on to the lawn tomorrow if the weather holds . . . The cushion covers have washed well . . . I'll wash the curtains this afternoon . . .

A sound from the next room cut sharply through her mellow dreams of curtain washing and carpet sweeping. She stood motionless, listening, an anxious frown on her face. Another sound came from the next room. The peace that had enveloped the house was shattered. William had not gone for a nice little walk.

Heaving a sigh, she went into the dining-room. William was scattering the last particles of a packet of tea upon the carpet.

'Well, you can't say I've not done *this* all right,' he said virtuously, as he screwed up the empty packet and threw it into the fireplace. 'I heard ole Mrs Mexton talkin' to someone an' she said there was nothin' like the old-fashioned way of cleanin' a carpet with tea-leaves. She said it was better than all these modern machines an' suchlike an'—'

'William!' gasped Mrs Brown. 'She meant *used* tea-leaves and even *they*'re no use. What a frightful mess you've made!'

William flung out his arms in an eloquent gesture.

'Well, that's what she *said*. She said there was nothin' like the old-fashioned way of cleanin' a carpet with tea-leaves. She—'

'It's going to take me *hours* to get it out.'

'But I only did the same as she *said*. How was I to know she meant you'd got to make tea of 'em first? She never *said* so. She never *said* make tea of 'em first . . . Tell you what!' The frown cleared from his brow. 'We could pour boilin' water on 'em on the carpet. *That*'d make 'em into used tea-leaves all right.'

'No, William. You've made enough mess already.'

William repeated his eloquent gesture.

'But I keep tellin' you I only did what she *said*. She said there was nothin' like the old-fashioned way of cleanin' a carpet with tea-leaves.'

Mrs Brown raised her hand to her head.

'William, will you *stop* saying that!'

'Well, *she* said it. It wasn't me that said it. It was *her*. She said there was nothin'—'

'Will you go *out*, William!'

'Yes, but listen,' said William earnestly. 'While I was doin' those tea-leaves, I thought of a new way of cleanin' the 'flues. You've never let me do 'em before, but I thought with it bein' spring-cleanin' it'd save you time if I did it . . . I mean – well, I mean I thought you'd *like* me to do it.'

'William,' said Mrs Brown, controlling herself with difficulty, 'there's only one thing I'd like you to do and that is go out for a nice little walk.'

'All right,' said William despondently. 'But I bet you'll be sorry you didn't let me help with those 'flues. I bet you'll never think of the new way I've thought of. An' she just said *tea*-leaves. She didn't say make tea of 'em first. She—'

'*William!*'

'All right. I'm goin'.' He assumed an air of pathos. 'Turning your own son out like a dog! An' I don't b'lieve there's any *use* in spring-cleaning anyway. I b'lieve—'

He found himself addressing the empty air. Mrs Brown had returned to the comparative peace of her spring-cleaning chaos.

He wandered down the road dejectedly, hands in pockets, head sunk between his shoulders.

'She jus' said *tea*-leaves,' he muttered. 'How was I to know she meant make tea of 'em first? ... An' I *bet* I'd have cleaned those 'flues all right. Some people don't seem to *want* people to help 'em. It's enough to make people stop helpin' people all the rest of people's lives.'

But it was not in William's nature to remain downcast for long. Gradually his head emerged from his shoulders, his walk assumed its usual elasticity and he began to take an interest in his surroundings. There was a suspicious movement in the ditch that might have been made by a water-rat, two sparrows were carrying on a spirited fight in the hedge, a horse in a field on the other side of the hedge kicked up its heels suddenly and began to gallop across the field, and a man carrying a basket came suddenly round the bend in the road. William's interest, divided till now between water-rat, sparrow and horse, concentrated itself on the man who was walking with a long springing stride down the road. He was tall, thin, dark-skinned and bearded and he wore a turban.

Without a moment's hesitation William turned in his tracks and began to walk beside him, looking up at him with unconcealed curiosity. He had never yet walked down the road with a man wearing a turban and he wanted to enjoy the experience. The man returned his scrutiny. William's hasty inspection of the 'flues before he laid his plans for their cleaning had left its traces across his forehead and down one cheek.

'Your face is dirty,' said the man.

He had a high-pitched staccato voice and he hunched up his shoulders as he spoke.

'I've been spring-cleaning,' said William with dignity.

'Ha!' said the man. 'It is fantastic, the spring-cleaning. Only the mind of a woman could have devised so tortuous a way of wasting time, energy and money.'

'Yes, that's jolly good,' said William, impressed. 'I was tryin' to say that to my mother, but I couldn't think of as good words as yours an' anyway she wasn't listenin'. I'll try'n' remember what you said. It was jolly good.'

The man set the basket down in the road, brought a pipe and tobacco pouch from his pocket, scraped the last grain of tobacco from the pouch into his pipe and proceeded to light it. William transferred his attention to the basket. A small squeak came from it.

'Is there a cat in there?' he said.

The man shook his head.

'Mice?'

Again the man shook his head.

'Guinea-pig? I once had a guinea-pig that made a noise like that . . . Well, a bit like that.'

The man stooped down and opened the basket. A black face with large soft eyes looked up at him from a nest of woolly material.

'Gosh!' gasped William. 'A monkey!'

'A langur,' said the man. 'He feels the cold. I keep shawl round him.'

'*Gosh!*' gasped William again.

The man had closed the basket and was walking on down the road. William accompanied him, his eyes glued to the basket.

'Where are you takin' it?' he said.

THE MAN OPENED THE BASKET AND A BLACK FACE WITH
LARGE SOFT EYES LOOKED UP AT WILLIAM.

'To a gentleman's private zoo. He has wanted a langur for
long. I bring him.'

'What's its name?'

'Tito.'

'Can I carry the basket?'

'No.'

'Can I have another look at him?'

'No,' said the man, adding with frigid courtesy: 'There is
no need for me to take you further out of your way.'

'You're not doin',' William reassured him. 'I'm goin' the
way you're goin'.'

'But I am going to the station.'

'Well, that's where I'm goin',' said William promptly. 'It's a funny thing but that's where I'm goin'. I'm goin' a little walk 'cause of this spring-cleanin' an' it's jus' a nice little walk to the station. I bet I'd have felt like goin' a little walk to the station, anyway . . . What does it eat?'

'It eats specially prepared food,' said the man shortly. He had evidently had enough of William's company.

'I'll buy it from you if you'd like to sell it,' offered William. 'It'd save you the trouble of takin' it to this zoo. I've got nearly two shillin's left over from a tip an aunt gave me, so I bet I could buy it all right, an' I could look after it all right, too. I've looked after animals all my life. I've looked after dogs an' rabbits an' a guinea-pig an' – an' caterpillars an' – an' I once had had a c'lection of insects that was *famous*. Well, everyone round here knew about them. They nearly filled a box till most of 'em got out. A monkey'd be nothin' to me.'

'A langur,' said the man.

'I bet it'd learn to eat cabbage leaves an' lettuce leaves,' said William. 'I'd prepare 'em special same as you said. Or dog biscuits. I've got a packet of ants' eggs, too, left over from a goldfish.'

The man surveyed the landscape in an absent fashion and made no comment.

'It might *like* ants' eggs,' went on William. 'They might be its nat'ral food. There mus' be ants in the jungle.'

The man made no comment.

'I once fed a guinea-pig on ants' eggs,' continued William. 'It died but I don't think it died of ants' eggs. I think it died of some other disease.'

They reached the station. The man walked on to the platform. After a few moment's hesitation William followed him. A train drew in. The man entered a carriage. After a moment's hesitation William followed him.

'I'll jus' stay till it's time for the train to go,' he said. He put his ear to the basket, 'I can hear it breathin'. Let's have another look at it, shall we? Jus' to make sure it's all right.'

The man had taken out his tobacco pouch and an expression of consternation flashed into his thin brown face.

'My tobacco! I meant to buy more tobacco. There was a shop just outside the station. Your presence distracted me.' He looked from William to the basket in a harassed speculative fashion. 'Keep your eye on him just for a moment till I return. I will run quickly to the shop and back. I will be here again before the train goes.'

William watched the man run lightly down the platform and vanish through the exit. Almost immediately the guard waved his flag and the train began to steam slowly out of the station. William leaned out of the window . . . The turbaned figure was running wildly along the platform in its wake, waving its arms and shouting unintelligibly in a high-pitched voice. The train gathered speed. The shouting figure became a mere dot in the distance. The train turned a corner and the dot disappeared . . . William drew a deep breath and sat beside his charge. Cautiously he opened the basket and the little face looked up at him again with soft dark eyes and made friendly chattering sounds.

A thrill of pride and excitement swept over William as he closed the basket. He began to embellish the adventure in his mind in order to relate it more impressively to his friends . . . 'Well, this man, he said he'd got to do some shoppin' an' would I take this valu'ble monkey along for him to the train. He wouldn't have trusted anyone else with this valu'ble monkey, but soon as he saw me he knew I was the sort of boy that could be trusted with a valu'ble monkey . . . '

The train drew up at a station and it occurred to William for the first time to wonder whither he and his charge were bound. He looked at the label on the basket . . . Steedham. The next station but one.

Assuming the responsible air of a boy entrusted with a valuable monkey, he sat close to the basket, keeping one hand on it and occasionally leaning down to apply his ear to it and murmur encouraging words to the occupant.

'Good ole Tito . . . Good ole boy . . . How're you gettin' on, ole boy? . . . Cheer up, ole Tito . . . '

The langur made small noises in reply which William interpreted as expressions of friendliness and interest. The train wound slowly through the countryside and pulled up sleepily at Steedham station.

William took the basket and descended on to the platform.

Asked for his ticket, he gave a comparatively accurate account of what had happened. The porter scratched his head. It was a situation that had never before arisen in the whole course of his career, and he didn't know how to deal with it.

'You'll have to wait 'til the nex' train come in,' he said at last, 'and that's not till another hour.'

'All right,' said William.

He sat on the seat with his basket beside him for what seemed an interminable length of time. Then he got up and approached the porter.

'That train mus' be jolly late,' he said. 'It's more than an hour since I got here.'

'It's five minutes exact,' said the porter shortly.

It was at this point that an irresistible temptation swept over William. He wanted to walk down the road like the turbaned man, carelessly carrying a monkey in a basket. He'd be back at the station long before the train came in. He picked up the basket.

'Jus' goin' for a little walk,' he said airily to the porter.

The porter stood scratching his head in a fresh access of perplexity as William made his way through the barrier and out into the road.

There he walked with an elaborately long springing stride. He was tall and thin and dark-skinned and turbaned. He carried a monkey in a basket – a monkey that he had saved from the attack of a savage leopard in darkest Africa. Or perhaps darkest India. No . . . He reconstructed the story. He had taken a thorn from the monkey's foot in the jungle and later, when he was captured by cannibals and was just going to be eaten alive, the monkey had leaped down from a tree and gnawed through his bonds and ever since had been his inseparable companion. No . . . He thought of a better one still. He had rescued the monkey from a circus where he was being ill-treated, and already a gang of circus men – ruthless, cruel desperados – were on his track. He quickened his pace and glanced back warily over his shoulder. The circus men were not in sight . . . but perhaps they had taken a short cut across the countryside and were waiting for him at the next bend in the road. They would be heavily armed, of course. They would stick at nothing. They would probably kidnap both him and the monkey.

He stopped. He was passing a large gateway decorated with flags. Through the gateway he could see an extensive stretch of park-like grounds and behind the trees, the outline of a stately mansion.

A large notice announced 'Steedham Garden Fête,' and a trickle of people was going through the gate. William watched with interest. In the distance he could see a roundabout and a hoop-la stall. William always found roundabouts and hoop-la stalls irresistible. An idea occurred to him. He could throw off the gang of circus men – though already they were fading in the light of reality – enjoy a ride on the roundabout and a few throws at the hoop-la stall, and be back at the station before the turbaned man's train arrived.

He entered the grounds and wandered down a broad path towards the lawn from which came the heartening strains of the roundabout. Then he considered his basket . . . You couldn't go on a roundabout with a basket. He looked about him. There was a row of stalls under the trees by the edge of the lawn. One, piled high with an accumulation of junk, had a notice, 'Bring and Buy Stall.' It appeared to have neither customers nor stall holder. William approached it. Beneath it were several baskets not unlike the one he was carrying. He would leave his basket among them – no one would notice it – have his roundabout ride, then retrieve it and be waiting on the platform by the time the train came in. He wedged the basket as unobtrusively as possible between two others and set off at a run towards the roundabout.

Turning a bend in the path, he collided with a tall elderly monocled man who stood talking to a clergyman.

'Look where you're going, my boy,' said the monocled man.

'Sorry,' said William breathlessly as he plunged on to his goal.

'No manners, the young of today,' said the monocled man severely as he watched William's fleeing figure. 'No manners, no consideration, no courtesy, no chivalry, no respect for law and order.'

'Exactly, Sir Gervase,' said the clergyman. 'Different from our generation, indeed. I always think how kind of you it is to throw your grounds open to the public on this occasion.'

'A pleasure,' said Sir Gervase. 'A pleasure, I assure you.'

'You haven't included the private zoo this year. Perhaps as well.'

'Yes . . . Some of the animals are a little nervous and the children are apt to feed them on unsuitable diet . . . I'm expecting a fresh inmate this afternoon, by the way. A friend has sent me a langur from India and his agent is delivering it to me this afternoon. But I'm rather worried about my zoo.'

'Oh, dear! Why?'

'Well, it turns out there's an old right of way running through it. My father and the man who owned the adjoining property were old cronies – both keen fishermen – and my father gave him a right of way through these grounds. It's not been used for years, but now a nephew of this other chap has inherited the property and he's going to run up a building estate in Five Acre Meadow and he's claiming the right of way for his wretched lorries. Clean through my zoo. It'll ruin the place . . . I'm sure I once heard my father say that the right of way had been relinquished, but I can't find any proof of it. The solicitors have no record . . . Well, there the thing is and apparently I can't get round it. I'll even have to knock the walls down.'

'Distressing,' said the clergyman.

'I use a stronger word,' said Sir Gervase with an eagle flash of his blue eyes. 'A word hardly fit for your ears, my dear Vicar. Ah, here I think is the man who was bringing my langur but—'

The tall thin turbaned man was making his way through the crowd, his face wearing an expression of acute anguish.

'Sir Gervase, is it not?' he panted as he reached the two.

'Yes,' said Sir Gervase. 'Where's the langur?'

'It has been stolen,' said the man dramatically. 'Stolen from under my very eyes.'

'Good Lord!' said Sir Gervase. 'Who stole it?'

'A boy,' said the man. 'Young in years but dyed deep in crime. A boy with a dirty face.'

'A boy—' Sir Gervase and the clergyman looked at each other. 'Good Heavens! That boy who charged into us just now!'

'Dirt across his forehead and down a cheek.'

'That's the one!' said Sir Gervase. 'Come on! Let's look for the young scoundrel and you can tell us what happened as we go.'

A hasty search revealed no sign of the young scoundrel.

'I expect he is far away by now,' said the turbaned man with a shrug of his thin shoulders.

But William was not far away. In fact he was quite near,

WILLIAM BURROWED FRANTICALLY FOR HIS BASKET. IT
WASN'T THERE!

burrowing frantically beneath the Bring and Buy stall for his
basket. It wasn't there. It had vanished. There seemed to be
baskets of every shape and size, containing every conceivable
article from roller-skates to Bath buns, but *his* basket with its
precious occupant had vanished. His grimy face tense with horror, he rummaged on the stall itself, turning over household
stores, tea-cosies, Victorian ornaments and woolly toys . . . till
a woman in a pink jumper and fur stole accosted him indignantly.

'How *dare* you disarrange all our things like that?' she said.
'What on earth do you think you're doing?'

'Looking for a monkey,' said William desperately.

'Don't be impertinent,' said the woman. 'And go away. Go
away!'

The ferocity of her tone startled William so much that the
flat iron he was holding slipped from his grasp on to a punnet
of new-laid eggs and, aghast at this fresh damage, he fled
down a tree-bordered path, stopping when he found he was
not being pursued and looking up at the trees in the vain hope
of seeing the monkey there. He didn't see the monkey, but,
seated on the grass under a beech tree, with a basket between
them, were two middle-aged women. They were obviously

sisters, dressed alike in neat grey suits, except that one wore a brown beret and the other a blue beret.

But it was not on the women that William's widening eyes fastened themselves. It was on the basket. There was something familiar about the basket. So many baskets had he investigated as he burrowed beneath the Bring and Buy stall that his impressions had become a little blurred, but there was certainly something familiar about the basket. He approached the couple tentatively.

'I don't think that people have brought and bought as well as they did last year,' Blue Beret was saying, 'but it's always an interesting stall to help at . . . and now for lunch. An excellent idea of yours to bring a picnic lunch, dear.'

'Yes,' said Brown Beret with a little secret smile, 'and I've prepared a very *special* lunch. I'm not going to let you know what it is till I've opened the basket. It's a surprise.'

'I don't somehow remember the basket,' said Blue Beret, looking at it reflectively.

'Oh, yes, dear,' said Brown Beret carelessly. 'They're all alike, these baskets. We've got several in the boxroom you know. I went up and chose a largish one because of the special lunch I was making and—'

'Please—' panted William urgently.

'Go away, boy,' said Blue and Brown Beret simultaneously.

'Look at his *face*,' said Blue Beret dispassionately.

'Have you no manners, boy?' said Brown Beret. 'Go away . . . And now, dear, I'm going to open the basket and make your mouth water.'

Slowly she began to raise the lid.

'You'll adore every morsel of it. You'll—'

She gave a shrill scream as Tito sprang out of the basket, seized the brown beret from her head, and, his long tail swinging, shot up the beech tree and ran fleetly along an overhanging branch.

Shouts rose up from all sides. There was an excited rush of people to the foot of the beech tree.

'The langur!' shouted Sir Gervase.

'Tito!' screamed the turbaned man.

'Is this your idea of a joke, dear?' said Blue Beret plaintively.

Buzzing with excitement, the crowd surged along the path as Tito, pausing a moment to put the brown beret on his head, swung himself from branch to branch. Then a gasp went up. Tito had reached a branch that stretched to the mansion itself and, swinging to the end of it, leaped nimbly in through an open window and vanished from view.

Beyond control, the crowd surged in at the front door.

'He's come downstairs.'

'He's in the library.'

'He's on top of the bookcase.'

'I still don't understand it, dear. Did you *know* there was a monkey in the basket?'

The crowd poured into the library. There on top of the bookcase was Tito, prancing exultantly, chattering at the crowd. Then he began to take the leather-bound books from the top shelf and hurl them down upon the heads below. Receiving the impact of hard leather bindings, the heads began to withdraw. Only Sir Gervase held his ground, picking up the books one by one as they showered down on him. Several of the bindings came adrift from their moorings and he retrieved them tenderly.

'A unique collection,' he said, 'and the little devil's ruining it. Can't say I've ever read any of them myself, but there they've been ever since I can remember. My father thought the world of them.' He bent down to pick up a large tome with a rubbed morocco binding. 'Horace . . . My father was great on Horace. Read him in season and out of season. In the original, of course. He – Good Heavens! What's this?'

A folded paper had dropped from between the pages. He

picked it up and examined it. Even his monocle seemed to dance with excitement.

'Good *Lord*! It's some sort of legal document . . . Yes. Listen. The old chap relinquishes his right of way in return for the fishing rights in that part of the river that runs at the bottom of the grounds. Legal, all right. Signed, sealed and witnessed. Drawn up in the North of Scotland. I suppose the old chaps were having a fishing holiday there so no wonder the

TITO HURLED THE BOOKS FROM THE TOP SHELF ON TO
THE HEADS BELOW.

solicitor couldn't trace it. Well,' he turned to the turbaned
man, 'this is a good day's work.'

But the man in the turban wasn't interested. He was making
small caressing noises to the langur. At last the langur, as if
noticing him for the first time, jumped suddenly down from
the bookcase and flung itself into his arms, nestling affectionately against his shoulder.

Sir Gervase patted its head.

'So the little chap can have a nice quiet home in the zoo,
after all. No highways, no lorries. Ha, ha!'

'My Tito,' murmured the turbaned man. 'What you must
have suffered at the hands of that villain!'

Then he turned and saw William standing in the forefront
of the group of spectators. His hand shot out accusingly.

'The thief! The boy! The boy with the dirty face!'

Sir Gervase adjusted his monocle, which had come adrift during the proceedings, and inspected William with interest.

'Ah, yes . . . The boy with the dirty face. We have met before, I believe. And are you, my boy, responsible for all this?'

'W-well, in a sort of way,' said William hoarsely, looking round for escape. 'I mean, I can 'splain all about it . . . I mean, you see, it was like this—'

Sir Gervase raised his hand.

'Explanations are tedious,' he said. 'Let us leave it at that. Your activities have caused a certain amount of confusion. I am no deep student of character, but I should imagine that your activities usually do. However, I have to thank you for the discovery of a valuable legal document so we will draw a veil over the rest of the proceedings.'

'Me draw no veil,' said the turbaned man indignantly. 'He steal my Tito. He let him loose among the trees. He risk his precious life. He—'

He stopped. William had tactfully withdrawn and was forcing a way out through the crowd. At the door Blue Beret was still harping on her grievances.

'I said from the beginning that it looked a different sort of basket – I *knew* it was a different sort of basket – but you wouldn't listen.' Her eye fell on William and lit up with gloomy interest. 'The boy! The boy who was hanging round! I believe he knows something about it. I believe—'

But William was already making good his retreat down the drive.

He found his way to the station, bought a ticket with an air of assurance that left the porter speechless, saw the train just moving out of the platform, flung himself into a passing carriage, picked himself up, leaned out of the window, gave a dignified salute to the gaping porter and settled down for the journey.

As his mind went over the events of the afternoon, the memory that stood out most clearly was the memory of Tito prancing on the top of the bookcase and hurling books down on to the crowd below, and he was conscious of a deep almost irresistible longing to hurl books himself from the top of a bookcase on to a crowd below. He felt that life could never be quite complete till he had done it.

Reaching home, he sauntered into the sitting-room, where Mrs Brown was sewing a cushion into a cushion cover.

'They've washed much better than I thought they would,' she said complacently, 'Well, dear, did you have a nice little walk?'

'Yes, thank you,' said William. 'I took a valu'ble monkey in a basket to Steedham an' it got loose an' found a valu'ble legal document, so they didn't mind.'

'What nonsense you talk, dear!' said Mrs Brown placidly, as she fastened off a thread and plumped the cushion into shape. 'Yes, it looks almost as good as new . . . I really think I shall have finished the spring-cleaning by the end of the week.'

William hunched his shoulders and spoke in a high-pitched staccato voice.

'Only a woman could—' He hunted in his memory for the words the man in the turban had used, finally giving up the attempt and ending lamely, 'Well, anyway only a woman could have.'

'I've been thinking, dear,' said Mrs Brown.

She paused. During William's absence she had felt pangs of remorse. She had rejected William's well-meant offers of help. She was always rejecting William's well-meant offers of help. And always afterwards she felt pangs of remorse . . . Even over the tea-leaves he had meant well. She ought to have found some little job for him to do that he couldn't go wrong over. And while he was out on his little walk she thought she had found one.

'Yes?' said William.

'Well, dear, if you *really* want to help with the spring-cleaning, you might dust the books in the dining-room book-shelves. It's a nice quiet little job and will be a great help to me.'

A gleam came into William's eye. He would fetch Ginger and they would re-enact the scene. First he would be the monkey on the bookcase and Ginger the crowd below. Then Ginger could be the monkey on the bookcase and he'd be the crowd below . . . The crowd might retaliate and throw the books back. Yes, that would make the whole thing more exciting. It would make it into a sort of duel. He and Ginger were experts in duels. They had had duels with potatoes, rotten apples, lumps of coal and even Begonia Tubers . . . but they had never tried books before . . . He'd dust them properly, of course, he assured himself, sternly quelling the small stirrings of his conscience. He'd be helping with the spring-cleaning, all right. He'd put them all back in their places afterwards. Well, it would do them *good* to get thrown about a bit. It would take the dust off the inside of the pages. And they might find a valuable legal document . . .

'May I go and get Ginger to help?' he said.

'If you like, dear,' said Mrs Brown doubtfully. Misgivings had suddenly assailed her. 'But surely you can do it alone?'

'No, you can't,' said William. 'You've got to have two.'

'Well, you'll do it thoroughly, won't you?' said Mrs Brown. 'You'll take them all out?'

'Yes, we'll take 'em all out,' promised William.

'And wash your face and make a nice quiet job of it. The book dusting, I mean.' Her misgivings were increasing. 'Just take them out quietly one by one and—'

But William was already out of ear-shot, hastening down the road to summon his fellow campaigner to the fray.

Chapter 3

William the Tree-Dweller

'Well, we've not fixed up how to get to the moon yet,' said William.

'We've tried lots of ways,' Ginger reminded him.

The two, having been turned out of Ginger's house by Ginger's mother because she wanted to make a cake without fear of constant raids on the ingredients, were making their way slowly along the road to William's house.

'Yes, but none of them have come off,' said William. 'We've got to keep on tryin' till somethin' does come off. Somethin's sure to come off sooner or later. Stands to reason it will. That's what happened to all the inventors in hist'ry. They went on tryin' an' tryin' an' in the end it came off.'

'Yes, but you don't know about all the ones that tried an' tried an' tried an' it didn't come off.'

'That's right! Keep on makin' objections!' said William irritably. 'Here I am tryin' to help civ'lisation an' the yuman race by gettin' them to the moon an' all you can do is to keep on makin' objections.'

'Well, you've got to have a rocket to get to the moon,' said Ginger, 'an' we've not got one.'

'I don't think a rocket's all that necess'ry,' said William after a moment's consideration. 'They've kept tryin' with it an' they've not done it yet. I shouldn't be surprised if this fuel they're usin' isn't too strong. It prob'ly goes too far. It prob'ly goes *miles* farther than the moon an' that's no good. They'll end by smashin' up the moon altogether an' then no one can get to it.'

'Well, what ought they to use?' said Ginger.

'I've been thinkin' . . . I think they ought to start with somethin' quite small an' sort of work their way up gradual to big things . . . You know, I can shoot a t'riffic distance with that new bow an' arrow of mine.'

'Well, you couldn't get to the moon with a bow an' arrow.'

'I never said you could,' said William. 'You jus' don't wait to see what I'm goin' to say. You start makin' objections the moment I open my mouth. You'd never get anythin' done for civ'lisation an' the yuman race if everyone started makin' objections the minute anyone else opened their mouth. Well' – with heavy sarcasm – 'it's news to *me* if you'd get anythin' done for civ'lisation an' the yuman race if everyone started makin' objections the minute anyone else opened their mouth.'

'Oh, all right,' said Ginger. 'Go on.'

'Well,' said William, 'I shouldn't be surprised if that las' shot of mine didn't get half way to the moon – well, quarter, anyway – an' what I thought was if we had somethin' that'd sort of give it an extra shoot – I mean somethin' on *top* of its ordin'ry shoot . . . '

'What?' said Ginger, adding in a slightly belligerent tone, 'Well, you can't say I'm makin' objections when I jus' say "what?", can you?'

'No, that's all right,' said William kindly. 'I don't mind ordinary questions . . . Well, what I thought was that if we could get a specially strong firework an' fix it to the end of this new arrow of mine an' let it off – the firework, I mean – jus' when I'm shootin' off the arrow, it'd go up jolly high an' then when we'd got into the way of it we'd put another firework on an' then another an' then another an' so on till we'd got it strong enough to get there.'

'Um-m-m-m,' said Ginger dubiously. 'Where do we get the fireworks?' adding, 'Well, *that's* an ordin'ry question, isn't it?'

'Oh, yes, that's all right,' said William. 'Well, it's the Fifth of November nex' week so there ought to be lots of fireworks about. My father gen'rally gives me a box of fireworks but he doesn't gen'rally give it to me till the axshull day an' we want to start this shootin' business straight off.'

'Ask him to let you have jus' one today. He might be in a good temper.'

'He's not in a good temper,' said William. 'He's in a bad temper 'cause of Mr Redditch.'

Mr Redditch had recently come to live near the Browns. He was a boastful, self-important little man to whom Mr Brown had taken an immediate and not unjustifiable dislike. Mr Redditch had joined the golf club of which Mr Brown was a member and had first earned his dislike by taking advantage of a convenient stroke to appropriate to his use a treasured new ball of Mr Brown's, leaving to Mr Brown a weary veteran of his own . . . and he continued to earn it by holding up the entire course while he knelt down to his putts and generally took his ease on the fairway.

Moreover, he went to London by the same train and generally in the same compartment as Mr Brown and dispelled his morning peace by incessant prattle. He talked of himself – his cleverness, his popularity, his outstanding ability in every field of life. He told rambling pointless stories, all redounding in one way or another to his own credit. No longer could Mr Brown read his morning paper from end to end during his morning journey up to town. Exasperation prevented his reading even two consecutive sentences.

And Mr Redditch's enormities did not end there. He insisted on having the window shut, whatever the weather;

he pushed his way into the railway carriage in front of Mr Brown in order to secure Mr Brown's favourite corner seat; having watched Mr Brown playing bridge at the golf club one wet afternoon, he spent the next morning's journey telling him of his mistakes. Mr Brown's irritation was gathering strength and his family began to look forward with trepidation to his evening return from work. Furthermore, Mr Redditch had taken to borrowing garden implements, seizing the opportunity when Mr Brown was out of the house and Mrs Brown's pliant amiability made her an easy prey.

'What's Mr Redditch got to do with it?' said Ginger.

'He makes him mad,' said William simply. 'Gosh! He was mad when he came home yesterday an' found he'd borrowed the saw.'

'You could try him,' said Ginger.

'Yes, I'll try him,' said William. 'I bet he wouldn't give me one jus' to mess about with, but if I explain that we're doin' 'speriments for civ'lisation an' the yuman race—'

'Yes, circumstances alter cases,' said Ginger, adding self-consciously, 'I read that in a book. It means the same as what you said but it's better English.'

'There's nothin' wrong with my English,' said William with spirit. 'I can talk it, can't I, an' no one can do more with it than that. That's what it's *for*, isn't it?'

'All right,' said Ginger. They had reached the gate of the Brown's homestead. 'Well, go in an' ask him.'

'All right. I'll go in an' ask him,' said William, something of his self-confidence oozing away from him as he spoke.

'Well, go on.'

'All right,' said William testily. 'Give me time to *breathe*.'

He walked up to the front door with a gait that held a mixture of swagger and reluctance – the reluctance predominating as he neared the door. He hesitated for a few moments, then vanished inside . . . to return almost immediately after-wards, looking heated and outraged.

'Wouldn't even listen to me,' he said. 'Jus' shouted "No!" at me. Wouldn't even let me explain. Jus' shouted "No!" at me again. He was still mad about that saw an' because this Mr Redditch had been tellin' him what was wrong with his golf. Gosh! Fancy anyone tellin' him there was anythin' wrong with his golf! Why, he's won *spoons* for golf . . . Anyway, my mother said I'd better get out, so I did. He'd have started bein' vi'lent in another minute.'

'Well, what are we goin' to do now?' said Ginger.

'An' me only tryin' to help sci'nce an' civ'lisation an' the yuman race!' said William, throwing his arms out in an eloquent gesture. 'Jus' gettin' shouted "No!" at when all I'm tryin' to do is help sci'nce an' civ'lisation an' the yuman race!'

'I suppose he jus' thought you wanted a firework,' said Ginger mildly.

'I tried to tell him, but he wouldn't listen.'

'Well, come on. Let's try mine.'

Though Ginger's father proved as unaccommodating as Mr Brown, an uncle of Ginger's, who had just returned from a city luncheon and was taking a more mellowed view of life, produced the sum of five shillings and sixpence which, in its turn, produced a formidable-looking rocket in a brightly-coloured wrapper.

They made their way back to William's garden. There, when William had fetched his bow and arrow from his bed-room and a box of matches from the top of the kitchen stove, they selected the middle of the lawn as the scene of the great experiment.

'That'll give us enough room jus' to start with,' said William. 'When we get to usin' six or seven of them we'll need a bigger place of course. P'raps if it's a success the government'll give us an airfield for it . . . Now we'll fix the rocket to the end of the arrow an' you light the rocket the same time I shoot off the arrow . . . Gosh! I shouldn't be s'prised if it makes a supersonic bang.'

They fixed the rocket on to the end of the arrow and William stretched the bow to its utmost length.

'Now you light a match,' he said 'an' put it to the rocket an' the minute it catches I'll let off the arrow. Now wait . . . One . . . Two . . . Three . . . *Go!*'

They had not seen William's father coming down the garden path, his brow wreathed in thunder-clouds of wrath, carrying in his hand what was left of the saw recently borrowed by Mr Redditch. He had only just discovered it, propped up inside the garden gate, returned without ceremony or acknowledgement or thanks, the edges flattened, the blade bent and distorted. It was evident that as a sawer of logs Mr Redditch belonged to the amateur class. Mr Brown was fuming with inward rage as he carried his maimed treasure towards the tool-shed. He was composing the highly-coloured speech that he would deliver to Mr Redditch at their next meeting. The fact that Mr Redditch had gone away for a week's holiday and that he could not immediately give vent to his eloquence added fuel to the fire of his wrath.

Culling his choicest flowers of rhetoric and invective, he did not notice the two boys on the lawn till William's strident '*Go!*' cut sharply through the air. Then he turned . . . to receive a smouldering, sputtering rocket full in the stomach with such force that he sat down heavily on the ground, while the saw performed a semi-circle in the air and came to rest in the middle of a rose-bush.

He flung the rocket aside and rose slowly and ponderously to his feet. His face was a beetroot hue and he was breathing heavily. It was clear that emotion had temporarily deprived him of the power of speech but it was equally clear that when the power of speech returned it would be both pointed and pungent. William hastened to make the most of the short time at his disposal.

'We didn't mean to do that,' he said. 'I'm sorry. We didn't *mean* to do it . . . Listen . . . We fixed the rocket on to the end of the arrow an' we meant it to go *with* the arrow. We didn't know it would come loose an' go straight for you like what it did. We didn't *know* it would. We didn't *mean* it to. We—'

Mr Brown had recovered the power of speech but was tempering it with iron self-control.

'Give me that bow and arrow,' he said.

William handed him the bow and Ginger retrieved the arrow from a potted Hydrangea and brought it to him.

'I shall destroy this,' said Mr Brown grimly, 'and I shall never allow you to have a bow and arrow again. Do you understand?'

'But—'

'Be quiet! Have you any more of those – those fireworks?'

'No, but—'

'And you shan't have any. You're to have no more fireworks. Please understand that. If you have any given you I shall confiscate them.'

'But, Dad, it's Guy Fawkes day nex' week.'

'I'm quite aware of that,' said Mr Brown, bending down to rub his ankle, which had got slightly twisted in his fall, 'and you're to have no fireworks for it. Nor are you to attend any firework display.'

'But, Dad,' pleaded William, 'it's – it's a sort of *juty* to have fireworks on Guy Fawkes day. This Guy Fawkes man, he – he—' William had always been a little vague as to the exact role played by Guy Fawkes in history. 'He tried to save the country from havin' a Parliament. We ought to celebrate him same as we do Nelson an' St. George an' – an' Dick Turpin an' all the others. It's our *juty* to.' He searched wildly for some reason that would appeal to his father. 'I bet people'll think I'm a communist if I don't have fireworks on Guy Fawkes day. I bet I'll get put in prison for a communist an'—'

'Be *quiet!*' said Mr Brown. He drew a deep breath and continued, 'Haven't you any sense at all? Are you a complete and utter imbecile? Haven't you any ideas in your head but tomfoolery and wanton destruction? You aren't fit to be a member of a civilised community and you seem to grow less fit with every day that passes. If you choose to go playing the fool, damaging property and endangering the life and limb of everyone around you, you must take the consequences.'

'Yes, but listen, Dad,' said William. 'I wasn't playin' the fool. I was doin' a sci'ntific experiment for civ'lisation an' the yuman race. If I'd jus' been playin' the fool, I wouldn't mind takin' what you said, but with it bein' a sci'ntific experiment makes it diff'rent.'

'Circumstances alter cases,' murmured Ginger, coming to the help of his friend as best he could.

'Be *quiet!*' roared Mr Brown, 'and be off, both of you!'

'But, Dad,' began William, standing his ground till Mr Brown advanced on him, the light of purpose in his eye, then beating a hasty retreat, scrambling through the hedge with Ginger at his heels.

'Gosh!' he panted when he reached the safety of the road. 'He jus' wouldn't listen an' – Gosh! No fireworks on Guy Fawkes day!'

'We ought to've tied it tighter,' said Ginger.

But William was less interested in his experiment than in his grievances.

'Jus' sat down ordin'ry an' didn't hurt himself at all . . . Why, there's people that have given their *lives* for sci'ntific experiments – atom bombs an' radium an' suchlike – without makin' as much fuss as he made jus' sittin' down ordin'ry. Some people'd be *int'rested* in sci'ntific experiments an' gettin' to the moon, but he didn't seem to be. No,' – with his short sarcastic laugh – 'I mus' say *he* didn't seem to be int'rested in them. Jus' went on at me as if I was a crim'nal. There's some people that'd be proud to have people in their fam'lies that did sci'ntific experiments for civ'lisation an' the yuman race. Gosh! It isn't a *crime* to try'n' help civ'lisation an' the yuman race. Well, it's news to *me* if it is. It's news to *me* if it's a crime to try'n' help civ'lisation an' the yuman race. It—'

'Well, how are we goin' to manage without fireworks?' said Ginger, hastening to stem the tide of William's eloquence before it reached flood proportions. 'I bet my uncle won't give me any more.'

'Gosh! didn't he carry on!' said William, who was never easily diverted from his theme. 'Sayin' I wasn't fit to be a member of a civ'lised community! Well, I jolly well don't *want* to be a member of one. I'm jolly well *sick* of civ'lised communities. I'm jolly well *sick* of tryin' to help civ'lisation an' the yuman race. All I get for it is my bow an' arrow took off me an' no fireworks. That *shows* civ'lisation's all wrong an' I'm jus' about fed up with it. I'm jolly well goin' back to the days before there *was* any civ'lisation. I bet everyone was a jolly sight better off before it started. I bet we'd all be a jolly sight better off if we all went back to bein' savages same as those ole Markie was tellin' us about that lived in trees.'

'Tree-dwellers,' said Ginger.

'Yes, them . . . Well, I'm jolly well goin' back to bein' one. I'd sooner live in a tree than a house any day. Gosh!' – his gloom lightened as he warmed to his new theme – 'an' we *could*, too! There's lots of trees round here. We could start bein' tree-dwellers straight away an' I bet it'd sort of set the fashion an' everyone'd start doin' it an' it'd be the end of civ'lisation an' a jolly good thing, too!'

'I dunno that *everyone*'d want to live in trees,' said Ginger thoughtfully.

'I don't see why not,' said William. 'They're always grumblin' what a lot their houses cost them. Rates an' things. An' trees are *free*, aren't they? Well, it's news to *me* if trees aren't free.'

'The rain'd come in.'

'You could fix somethin' up to keep the rain off. An' they're jolly comfortable, are trees, 'cause I've tried 'em. They wouldn't need furniture if they got the right sort of tree. There's branches that make jolly good tables an' chairs. You could have meals in 'em. I've et lots of things in trees an' they tasted a jolly sight nicer than the things you eat in houses. I—' He stopped suddenly. They were passing a house in the garden of which grew a tree with broad spreading branches. 'That looks a good one. I'd like to try that one.'

'Gosh, you can't, William. Someone lives there.'

'Well, I keep tellin' you trees are free. Come to that, the whole earth's free for savages, so now we've started bein' savages the whole earth's free to us.'

Ginger considered this argument with frowning brows. It seemed unanswerable.

'Well, I dunno . . . ' he said at last.

'There's no one about, anyway,' said William. 'An' no one'll see us once we're in it. We can use it for practice an' then when we've found out how it works we can go an' find an impenetrable forest to tree-dwell in.'

'Yes, but—' began Ginger and stopped.

William had already crossed the lawn and, after an agile leap, was dangling by his hands from the lowest branch. Ginger hesitated a moment then followed him.

'It's a jolly easy tree,' came William's voice from beyond the first two branches. 'It's jus' like a ladder. You go up an' up as easy as easy. Come on.'

Ginger swung his solid form on to the lowest branch and began to scramble from branch to branch. He found William comfortably ensconced on a branch near the top.

'This is a jolly good branch,' said William. 'I think I could sleep on this one. Look! I can stretch my legs out on it an' lean against the trunk. An' you could have the one opposite. It's nearly the same shape. An' the one underneath would make a good table. We could put things on it an'—'

The door of the house opened and a voice called:

'Tinker!'

'Gosh! That's Miss Hopkins,' whispered Ginger. 'I forgot she lived here. She lives here with her sister. An' that ole Tinker's her cat.'

'Well, let's stay quite still,' said William. 'She can't see us 'cause of the leaves an' she'll soon go in.'

'Tinker! Tinker! Tinker! Tinker! Tinker! Tinker! TINKER! What *can* have happened to him?'

Another voice answered. Evidently Miss Hopkins' sister had joined her in the garden.

'Perhaps he's up the tree, dear. He does sometimes go up the tree, you know.'

'Well, if he's up the tree we won't worry about him. He can get up and down quite easily.'

'Miaow!' cried William raucously.

It was his instinctive reaction to the suggestion that if Tinker was in the tree no further investigations would be made. He realised as soon as he had uttered the sound that it was a mistake.

There was a sudden silence.

'He is in the tree,' said one voice, 'and I think I can see him. I can see *something*.'

'It didn't sound like Tinker,' said the other.

'It must have been Tinker.'

'I'm worried, dear,' said the first voice. 'I wish it had sounded more like Tinker.'

'Miaow!' said William, trying to sound more like Tinker.

'It *is* Tinker,' said the second voice, 'but he doesn't sound himself somehow.'

'No, there was a note in it almost as if he were in distress . . . Or in pain.'

'Certainly upset about something.'

'Let's get a saucer of milk and put it at the foot of the tree. He may see it and come down.'

Their footsteps retreated to the house.

'Gosh! You've been an' done it now!' said Ginger. 'I s'pose you'll go down an' lap up the milk.'

'Oh, shut up,' said William, adding in a tone of disgust as his mind went back over various incidents in the past, 'I *would* be a cat! Cats! The muddles I've got into over cats! I've never had any luck with them.'

'Here's the milk,' said a voice from below.

'Put it right against the trunk, dear, where he can see it. Let's wait and see if he comes down.'

'What we've got to do now,' whispered William, 'is to make 'em think it's *not* a cat in the tree. Let's try'n' think of somethin'.'

It was at this point that Ginger lost his head, raising his voice in a hoarse bark. 'Bow-wow-wow!'

'Oh, *listen*!' screamed Miss Hopkins. 'He's groaning.'

'It sounded more like a cough to me. He must have got another attack of bronchitis, poor darling!'

'You chump!' whispered William. 'You don't have dogs in trees. Let's be birds quick!'

A clamorous squawking rang out from the shelter of the leaves . . . and Miss Hopkins gave another little scream of dismay.

'He's getting hysterical. He must be in the most dreadful pain. Let's ring up the vet at once.'

'We'll have to get him down first. We can hardly expect the vet to climb the tree to examine him.'

'What about borrowing Mr Redditch's ladder?'

'He's gone away, dear, and we don't know where it is . . . No, I've got a better idea. I'll get the clothes-line prop and *prod* him down and you must stand ready to catch him.'

'Hold on tight!' whispered William.

'Let's try'n' do somethin' to frighten them,' said Ginger. 'I bet I could roar like a lion. I – *Ow!*'

A long narrow pole had appeared suddenly through the branches and caught him violently in the chest. He grabbed hold of William. Both lost their balance and crashed through the branches to the ground. The Misses Hopkins stared in incredulous amazement at the sudden descent of two grubby small boys from the tree. Then the elder one pointed an accusing finger.

'So *you* are the boys who have been *torturing* our poor darling Tinker up in that tree.'

'No, we haven't,' said William indignantly as he scrambled to his feet. 'We haven't been torchering anything up in that tree. We've *been* torchered, more like. We—'

'Don't dare to deny it,' snapped Miss Hopkins. 'We heard the poor dumb creature's groans and cries for help.'

'It wasn't,' said Ginger. 'It was dogs an' birds an'—'

'Trespassing in our garden, and torturing our cat!' said Miss Hopkins, her voice trembling with passion. 'We'll see what your father has to say about it.'

She came towards them, brandishing the clothes prop and, for the second time that day, William and Ginger chose discretion as the better part of valour, plunging out of the gate . . . down the road . . . and in at another gate that stood conveniently open.

MISS HOPKINS ADVANCED UPON THEM,
BRANDISHING THE CLOTHES PROP.

'We'll hide in here 'case she's comin' after us,' said
William, taking refuge behind a Rhododendron bush.

'She's not comin' after us,' panted Ginger, 'but she was
standin' at the gate an' saw us come in.'

'Oh, well, it's all right if she's not comin' after us,' said
William, emerging from his hiding-place and looking about
him. 'Gosh! *That*'s a good tree.'

'You're not goin' to go *on* with it, are you, William?' said
Ginger. 'Tree-dwellin', I mean. Not after all that!'

''Course I am,' said William, walking round the tree and
looking up at it in a speculative fashion. 'I said I was goin' to

be a tree-dweller an' I'm jolly well goin' to *be* one. I'm not goin' to be put off by a little thing like that. If I'm goin' to get into a row for trespassin' in one garden, I might as well get into one for trespassin' in two. Anyway, this is Mr Redditch's garden an' he's gone away so *he* can't come out an' say we're torcherin' his cat. I chose it for hidin' in 'cause I knew it was Mr Redditch's an' I thought it'd be a good place with him bein' away. I didn't know there was such a jolly good tree in it as this one. Look at it! It's easier even than the one in ole Miss Hopkins' garden . . . '

'Well, I think we've done enough for one day,' said Ginger.

'All right,' said William. 'You go home. I'm goin' to stay an' have a shot at it. I mayn't ever get such a good tree for practicin' tree-dwellin' in all the rest of my life.' He had already manipulated the lowest branch and his voice came muted through the leafage.

'No, I'll stay with you,' said Ginger resignedly as he made ready to follow his leader.

In a few minutes they had reached a broad flattish branch near the top of the tree.

'Gosh, this is a smashing one,' said William. 'I bet it's more comfortable than lots of ordin'ry beds. I—'

'Someone's comin' in at the gate,' said Ginger in an urgent whisper.

William peered through the branches. A muffled figure had entered the gate and was making its way in the shadow of the bushes towards the house. Though dusk was falling, William plainly recognised the pursed, pallid features of Mr Redditch.

'Gosh!' he whispered apprehensively, but Mr Redditch, his face lowered, his shoulders hunched, had passed safely beneath the tree.

Then began so strange a performance that William nearly lost his balance from sheer amazement. For Mr Redditch approached the window of his house and, taking from his pocket a largish implement wrapped in a cloth, deliberately broke one of the panes, put his hand through the broken glass and slipped back the catch. He gave a stifled exclamation as he did so and they saw him take out his handkerchief and wrap it round his hand. Then slowly he raised the window and lifted one leg over the sill, catching his raincoat on a nail of the trellis fixed to the wall and tearing a hole in the lining. He gave another stifled exclamation – this time of annoyance – clutched the coat about him, lifted the other leg over the sill and vanished from sight.

'What's he doin'?' said Ginger. 'I thought he'd gone away.'

'I 'spect he's come back for somethin' an' forgotten his key,' said William. 'I bet I could have found a way in for him if he'd asked me. What's he doin' now? Can you see?'

They edged their way along the branch and craned their necks till they could see through the window. And there a yet stranger sight met their eyes. For Mr Redditch was opening drawers and cupboards and strewing their contents on the floor till the carpet was almost hidden by them.

'Crumbs!' said William. 'The things grown-ups can do without gettin' into rows! I'd get into a row all right if I made all that mess in a room. He's not even put the drawers back . . . an' he's not found what he's lookin' for yet. An' he's goin' out of the room without even botherin' to clear it up.'

'Wonder what it is he's forgotten,' said Ginger.

'P'raps it's his camera. P'raps he wants to take some snapshots on his holiday same as people do an' he's left his camera behind an' so he had to come back for it.'

'Or it might be his pyjamas.'

'Or his money.'

'Or his fountain pen.'

'Or his watch.'

'Or his lighter.'

'Or his bath sponge,' said Ginger a little feebly.

At this point their imagination flagged and they turned their attention to the house again.

'There he is!' said William excitedly as a figure quickly passed an upstairs window. 'He's not found it yet.'

'*Might* be his bath sponge,' said Ginger, who felt that this suggestion needed a little bolstering up. 'He might want a bath after his journey and find he'd forgot his sponge an' it might be early closin' day where he's gone to so he couldn't buy another so he's had to come back for it.'

'An' forgot his key.'

'Yes.'

'Look! He's come downstairs again. He's in the dining-room now. Let's get on that next branch an' see what he's doin'.'

They removed themselves to the next branch and the manoeuvre was rewarded by another strange spectacle, for Mr Redditch was revealed in the act of taking an assortment of silver from a cupboard and packing it carefully into a suit-case.

'Fancy comin' all the way back for that!' said Ginger.

'P'raps it's his birthday tomorrow an' he wants to have a party,' suggested William. 'Grown-up people always want to use posh things at parties. They haven't any *sense* at all . . .' His eyes wandered round the room and widened still further in surprise. For there, too, drawers and cupboards had been opened and their contents tossed on to the floor. 'Well, I'm glad he's found what he came back for, but I never saw any-one make such a muddle lookin' for anythin' before. Gosh! I wish my mother could see it. She'd never call *me* untidy again.'

'I bet she would,' said Ginger.

Mr Redditch, throwing a last glance round the room, was making his way out of it. They waited expectantly for his reappearance at door or window but nothing happened. He could not be seen at any of the windows. He did not emerge from the front door.

'I b'lieve he's in the back garden,' whispered William. 'I b'lieve I heard somethin' . . . Come on. Let's have a look.'

They climbed down the tree and crept round the corner of the house . . . to witness the most mysterious happenings of the whole mysterious evening. For Mr Redditch was engaged in digging a hole in his vegetable patch between a row of runner beans and a row of celery. Having dug the hole, he put the suitcase into it and covered it with soil. Then he dug another hole and, taking a pair of shoes from his pocket, proceeded to bury them, covering them over with soil and carefully forking over the surface of the surrounding soil to hide all traces of his cache. Then he put the fork into the tool-shed and made his way furtively round the side of the house, past the Rhododendron bush behind which the boys had taken cover and out again into the road.

MR REDDITCH DUG A HOLE AND PUT THE SUIT-CASE INTO IT.

William and Ginger emerged from the bush and stared at each other.

'*Well!*' said Ginger. 'What did he do that for?'

William considered. There were few situations that William could not explain to his own – if to no one else's – satisfaction.

'I bet I know,' he said. 'They're valu'ble things an' when he went on this holiday he got worried 'case someone stole them so he thought he'd come back an' hide them an' he did, but he'd forgot his key so he had to break a window.'

Ginger considered this.

'Funny place to hide 'em,' he said at last.

'Y-yes,' agreed William. 'They'll get jolly wet if it rains. But I s'pose he thought thieves'd never think of diggin' up a garden. It was jolly clever in a way.'

'What about his shoes? Why did he bury his shoes?'

'Well . . . p'raps he was fond of them an' didn't want them to get stolen. P'raps he'd gone mountaineerin' in them. People *do* get fond of boots an' shoes they do things in. Robert makes an awful fuss about his rugger boots an' so does Ethel about the boots she's got her skates on.'

'I s'pose so,' said Ginger vaguely. He looked round at the gathering dusk. 'I guess it's about bedtime. We'd better go home.'

But William found it difficult to leave the place. Its fascination lay strong on him.

'Let's jus' have another look through the windows at all the muddle he's made,' he said.

They went round to the front of the house and, looking in through the windows, feasted their eyes on the open drawers and cupboards, and the littered carpets.

'Crumbs!' said William. 'I bet his mother would have somethin' to say to him if he'd got one. I wonder if he's left the upstairs rooms as bad.'

'We can't see the upstairs rooms,' said Ginger, 'so we don't know.'

William's eyes roved round and came to rest on a trellis to which a rose-tree clung half-heartedly.

'I bet I could get up an' have a look,' he said. 'After all that tree climbin' I've done a bit of trellis is nothin' to me.'

'Well, don't start tryin' to be a trellis-dweller,' said Ginger, chuckling at his own wit.

'Now watch me,' said William putting a foot in one of the trellis holes and swinging himself up.

His progress was slow. He was encumbered by rose-shoots, scratched by thorns and hampered by the narrow footing the trellis holes afforded but at last he gave a cry of triumph.

'I can see right into it now an' – an' – Gosh! it's jus' as bad as the others. *Gosh!* It's worse. Everythin' all over the floor an' – an' – ' His voice rose to a cry of 'Help!' as, with a harsh rending sound, the trellis collapsed beneath his weight and came crashing to the ground.

He crawled out of the débris – crowned with rose-shoots, festooned with bits of broken trellis – and picked himself up.

'Well, *now* you've done it,' said Ginger, staring aghast at the destruction that surrounded them, 'an' he'll *know* it was us 'cause Miss Hopkins saw us come in an' she'll tell him. Huh!' He gave a good imitation of William's sarcastic laugh. 'That bow an' arrow an' fireworks took away's goin' to be nothin' to what's goin' to happen to us now.'

William removed some rose-shoots from his hair and a piece of broken trellis from his foot, then stood for a few moments in an attitude of deep thought.

'*Tell* you what!' he said at last. 'If we could do somethin' to *help* Mr Redditch he might be so grateful he wouldn't mind about the old trellis.'

'What could we do?' jeered Ginger. 'You tell me *one* thing we could do.'

'All right, I will,' said William. 'I've got a jolly good idea. You know those things he dug into the garden to keep 'em in a safe place from thieves.'

'Yes?'

'Well, we could dig 'em up an' put them in a *really* safe place. That suit-case'll get ru'ned in the earth if it rains an' so will those shoes. If we dug 'em up an' hid 'em for him in my wardrobe at home instead, they'd be safer from thieves than in his garden *an'* they'd keep dry. Thieves might easy go dig-gin' about in his garden stealin' plants an' things an' find them. An' then when he comes home from his holiday we'll take 'em round to him dry an' safe, an' he'll be so grateful he won't say a word about the trellis . . . It's a jolly good idea, isn't it? Let's get the fork out and start.'

'I dunno that we ought . . . ' said Ginger.

WILLIAM AND GINGER MADE THEIR WAY DOWN THE ROAD
CARRYING THE SUIT-CASE BETWEEN THEM.

'Oh, come *on*,' said William, who was already opening the door of the tool-shed.

A few minutes later they were making their way down the road, carrying the suit-case between them, their trail marked by pieces of damp earth that dripped from the suit-case and odds and ends of trellis and climbing rose that detached themselves at intervals from William's person.

They slackened their pace in a slightly apprehensive manner when they reached William's house, but fortune seemed at last to be on their side. No one was about. Unchallenged and unimpeded they went up to William's bedroom and hid suit-case and shoes at the bottom of William's wardrobe. It was not till they were coming downstairs again that they met Mrs Brown in the hall.

'William!' she said. 'What a state you're in! Where *have* you been? It's *ages* past your bedtime. Your father's just come in and he says that if you aren't in bed by—'

She stopped. The two had vanished as at the wave of a magician's wand – William up to his bedroom and Ginger in the direction of his home.

The next morning William awoke to a confused memory of a crowded and eventful day. William frequently awoke to confused memories of crowded and eventful days but he had a vague idea that this one was more crowded and eventful than usual. Sitting up in bed, frowning thoughtfully, he sorted out the events as best he could. The bow and arrow . . . the rocket . . . his father's wrath . . . tree-dwelling in Miss Hopkin's garden . . . tree-dwelling in Mr Redditch's garden . . . the broken trellis . . . the rescue of Mr Redditch's goods.

He got out of bed and opened his wardrobe door . . . Yes, the suit-case and shoes were still there. He would be able to hand them over, safe and dry, to Mr Redditch on his return. So the broken trellis, at any rate, he thought optimistically, should not bring any complications in its train. There remained the tree-dwelling in Miss Hopkin's garden and the alleged torture of her cat.

He went downstairs and breakfasted heartily and in comparative silence, throwing wary glances at his father, who was, as usual, entrenched behind his newspaper. It was Saturday, so Mr Brown would be at home all day. An announcement that he would not be going to golf made William's heart sink. He had been consoling himself by improbable mental pictures of Miss Hopkins coming to complain to his father, finding him at golf, going home and forgetting all about her grievance.

'What are you going to do this morning, William?' said his mother.

He hesitated. Wisdom urged him to absent himself as far and as long as he could from the scene of possible retribution. Curiosity urged him to stay near at hand and watch events. There had always been more curiosity than wisdom in William's make-up.

'I'll jus' be messin' about in the garden,' he said.

'Don't mess too much,' said Mrs Brown with a smile, and Mr Brown gave a sardonic snort from behind his newspaper.

The first part of the morning passed without incident. William occupied himself in making paper darts and testing their aerial flights, keeping a watchful eye upon the road. Then – things began to happen.

First of all Miss Hopkins appeared, bringing in her train an obviously reluctant Mr Redditch. She had swept him up, ignored his protests and brought him along with her to demand an interview with Mr Brown.

William waited for the summons. It came.

'William! Come in here at once.'

William entered the sitting-room by the french windows. His father stood on the hearth-rug, the thunder-clouds again upon his brow. Miss Hopkins and Mr Redditch stood facing him.

'Torturing our cat up the tree!' Miss Hopkins was saying. 'Trespassing in our garden and torturing our cat up the tree! The poor thing was screaming with agony.'

'I wasn't torcherin' any ole cat,' said William indignantly. 'It was Ginger bein' a dog an' Ginger an' me bein' birds. They were jolly good birds an'—'

'Be quiet, William,' said Mr Brown. 'You'll have an opportunity of giving what explanation you can later.'

Miss Hopkins, who had merely stopped to draw breath, continued:

'And not content with trespassing in our garden, we saw him – *saw* him with our own *eyes* – go into Mr Redditch's garden and start trespassing in that. I thought that Mr Redditch was away—'

'I was away,' said Mr Redditch, 'but the police 'phoned for me to come back early this morning. They had found the house broken into and ransacked by burglars. *Ransacked.*'

'But—'

'Be quiet, William.'

'Tinker hasn't been home all night. He's not up the tree now. I can't think *what*'s happened to him.'

'Ransacked from top to bottom. Smart work of the police. They noticed the broken window and got into touch with me at once.'

'Yes, but listen. I—'

'Be *quiet*, William.'

'We could hear the poor darling mewing for help up that tree while those cruel boys—'

'All my Georgian silver gone. Not a piece left. A most valuable collection.'

'Yes, but—'

'Will you be *quiet*, William!'

'Most unfortunate having to return like this the first day of my holiday.'

'The sweetest disposition. He wouldn't hurt a fly. How those cruel boys had the heart to—'

'But listen. I—'

'An expert's job, the police think. Fortunately the stuff was insured but the mess they made in the house has to be seen to be believed.'

'We've had him since he was a kitten. He's never had a harsh word, and to be *tortured* by those boys up a tree . . . '

'If you'd jus' listen—'

'Be QUIET, William.'

'The police are there now looking for clues. I really oughtn't to have left the place, but Miss Hopkins insisted.'

'Of course I insisted.'

'A policeman's come, dear,' said Mrs Brown in a resigned tone of voice, opening the door to admit a stalwart form in blue.

'S'cuse me interrupting,' said the policeman. He looked at Mr Redditch. 'I heard you'd come here, sir, so I followed you.' He took a notebook from his pocket. 'I think I've got all the particulars now. Footmarks on the garden bed just below the window. Shoes with distinctive pattern on rubber sole. Large size. Twelve or thereabouts.' Mr Redditch glanced down at his own small neat feet. 'Window broken, of course. That's what first drew our attention to the fact that the premises had been entered. Trellis broken down.'

'I don't understand about the trellis,' said Mr Redditch with a puzzled expression, then stopped in confusion.

'Oh, that's quite simple, sir,' said the policeman. 'The thief intended to climb up to the bedroom window by the trellis and when it broke under his weight he smashed the downstairs window instead and slipped back the catch and got in that way. No fingermarks, of course – they all wear gloves these days – but plenty of footmarks on the parquet flooring indoors. A large man, as I said, wearing shoes size twelve or thereabouts. You're insured, sir, I hope?'

'Yes,' said Mr Redditch. 'Fortunately I'm insured.'

'Oh, dear!' said Mrs Brown. 'Here's someone else coming to the door. I'll go and open it.'

'If you'd jus' *listen*—' began William again.

'William,' said Mr Brown, 'once and for all, will you be *quiet*!'

Mrs Brown re-entered, followed by a tall keen-eyed young man.

'Good-morning,' said the young man in a business-like

tone of voice. 'I've just been to Mr Redditch's house and was told that he was here.'

'Yes, there he is,' said William, 'an' if you'd jus' let me—'

'*William!*' said Mr Brown.

'I represent the Mayflower Insurance Company,' said the young man, 'and, as I happened to be on a job over at Hadley, they asked me to come over and see you. I gather that you rang them up earlier this morning to report a theft.'

'Yes,' said Mr Redditch. 'I've had some very valuable pieces of Georgian silver stolen.'

'I've got 'em,' said William. 'I've got 'em all. I've got his shoes, too.'

'William, be—' began Mr Brown then stopped. 'What did you say?'

'I've got 'em,' said William. 'I've got his shoes an' all those pieces of George silver upstairs in my wardrobe.'

'Don't talk such nonsense,' said Mr Brown sternly.

'But I have,' persisted William. 'I've been tryin' to tell you an' you wouldn't listen. Me an' Ginger were bein' tree-dwellers in Mr Redditch's garden las' night an' we saw him come back an' break his window 'cause he'd forgot his key. He cut his hand doin' it.' Mr Redditch hastily tried to conceal the long red cut on his right hand. 'An' he tore the inside of his raincoat, too.' Mr Redditch made a movement as if to clutch his raincoat about him, but the man from the Insurance Company whipped it open, exposing a jagged three-cornered tear. 'Well, then he packed up these George silver things in a case an' buried 'em in the garden so they'd be safe from thieves an' he buried his shoes too 'cause he used to go mountaineerin' in them an' he didn't want them stole, an' Ginger an' me broke the trellis so we thought we'd dig up his George stuff an' shoes an' put 'em in a place where they wouldn't get wet if it rained an' then we thought he wouldn't mind about his trellis if he found we'd kept his George stuff an' shoes safe an' dry for him.'

'Will you stop talking this arrant nonsense!' thundered Mr Brown.

'A pack of fantastic rubbish!' sputtered Mr Redditch.

'One minute, one minute, one minute!' said the man from the Insurance Company. 'You say you've actually *got* the things, my boy?'

'Yes, an' I'll *show* you,' said William.

He plunged upstairs and plunged down again, holding the muddy suit-case in one hand and a pair of muddy shoes in the other. He opened the suit-case and poured a stream of silver on to the hearth-rug. They stared at it, open mouthed.

'There!' he said to Mr Redditch. 'It's all there. We've saved it for you – Ginger an' me. It rained las' night an' it might have got *soaked* if Ginger an' me hadn't saved it for you, so I bet you feel grateful to us an' won't mind about the trellis now, will you?'

The look that Mr Redditch turned on William expressed many things, but gratitude was not among them.

'This is your silver, Mr Redditch?' said the man from the Insurance Company.

'Yes,' said Mr Redditch.

'And the shoes?'

The man from the Insurance Company was examining the shoes. They were large – size twelve or thereabouts – and they had rubber soles marked in a distinctive fashion.

'They're them,' said the policeman.

Mr Redditch turned a putty-coloured face to him.

'I don't know anything about them,' he muttered.

'Strange!' said the man from the Insurance thoughtfully. 'Well, I take it you won't be making a claim now.'

Miss Hopkins, who was standing by the window, gave a sudden scream.

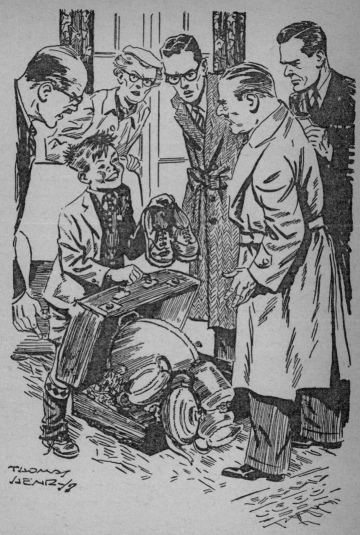

WILLIAM OPENED THE SUIT-CASE AND POURED A STREAM
OF SILVER ON TO THE HEARTH-RUG.

'There's my darling Tinker!' she said.

A large grey cat could be seen ambling in an airy fashion down the road, with tail erect.

She rushed out of the house and returned holding the fiercely protesting animal.

'There's the wretched boy, my darling,' she said, pointing at William. 'Oh, if my Tinker could *speak!*'

Her Tinker struggled out of her grasp, jumped on to the floor and went to William, purring and rubbing itself against his shoes.

'I don't think he'd have much to say, if he could,' said Mr Brown dryly.

In the diversion caused by Tinker's return, Mr Redditch had made a quiet and unobtrusive exit, bundling silver and shoes unceremoniously into his suit-case. The policeman followed. Miss Hopkins also followed, holding the struggling Tinker in her arms and cooing at him affectionately.

Mrs Brown drew a deep breath.

'*Well!*' she said. 'I think I'll make a cup of coffee.'

'You see,' the man from the Insurance Company explained to William, stirring his coffee thoughtfully, 'this chap staged a burglary because he wanted to get the insurance money. I suppose he'd have put in a pretty stiff claim and then – as likely as not – he would have sold the stuff as well. Do you understand?'

'Yes,' said William, adding zestfully – for William liked his drama laid on thick – 'He's prob'ly the head of a gang of international crim'nals. Prob'ly Scotland Yard have been huntin' for him for years. He's prob'ly a smuggler as well. An' a spy. He's prob'ly foiled the best brains in the Secret Service.'

'Well, hardly that I think,' said the man from the Insurance Company mildly, 'but the fact remains that you happen to have saved my company a tidy sum of money and I think that I can safely say that if there's anything in particular that you'd like as a reward we'd be willing to give it to you – within reasonable limits, of course.'

William threw a wary glance at his father, then turned a wooden, expressionless face to the man from the Insurance Company.

'I'd like a bow an' arrow an' a box of fireworks, please,' he said.

'Oh, William!' said Mrs Brown reproachfully. 'You know your father said—'

But Mr Brown waved the objection aside. The thunder-clouds had cleared from his brow. Life stretched before him again, free and unhampered. No longer would Mr Redditch poison his game of golf, shatter the peace of his morning journey to town, play havoc with his gardening implements. He even had a shrewd suspicion that Mr Redditch would soon be leaving the neighbourhood altogether.

'No, no, no, my dear,' he said genially. 'That's quite all right. Quite all right. As Ginger aptly put it, circumstances alter cases.'

Chapter 4

William and One
of Those Things

'Look at it!' said William, gazing at the small toy aeroplane in the shop window. 'An' only two bob!'

'It's a Gloster Meteor,' said Ginger, pressing his nose against the glass.

'Or a Vulcan.'

'Or a Hunter.'

'Or a Swift.'

'Anyway, it's wizard. We could have a Farnborough display with it.'

'Yes,' agreed William, 'if we'd got two bob, but we haven't. I haven't any money at all, have you?'

'No.'

William considered deeply for some moments, then said:

'Didn't you say you'd got to take your aunt's cat to the vet's this afternoon?'

'Yes,' said Ginger. 'It's had something wrong with its ear. It's all right now, but she wants me to take it to the vet so's he can *say* it's all right. She's bats on it.'

'Well, p'r'aps she'll give you a tip for takin' it,' said William.

'An' p'r'aps she won't,' said Ginger bitterly. 'She's never given me a tip for anythin' yet an' she's not likely to start today.' He too considered deeply for a few moments then went on, 'It's a long time since Robert gave you a tip.'

'Y-yes,' agreed William.

His thoughts went to his elder brother Robert, who was in his eyes the incarnation of tyranny, unreasonableness, ruthlessness and vindictiveness. On the other hand there was no denying that Robert had his better moments.

'He can't kill you,' encouraged Ginger.

'Can't he!' said William darkly. 'He nearly can. He nearly did that time I tried to mend the silencer on his motor-bike for him. I'd got it to pieces all right an' I bet I'd have got it together again all right if he'd let me go on with it. I'd taken out the thing that was makin' too much noise. At least I think I had.'

'Well, you've not done anythin' to make him mad lately, have you?'

'No, but someone else may have done somethin' to make him mad an' that comes to the same thing.'

'Well, let's try, anyway.'

'All right,' said William doubtfully. They began to walk slowly down the road. 'I bet it won't come off. It's a funny thing but I never seem to catch anyone in a good temper when I want them to give me money. It seems as if somethin' sort of *told* them I was goin' to ask them, so's they could get in a bad temper ready for it. Anyway, I don't know where he is. He went off to tennis an' I bet he won't be home yet an'—'

'There he is!' said Ginger.

Robert was just coming round the bend of the road, accompanied by a slender girl with blonde hair and eyes of periwinkle blue. They were evidently returning from the tennis club. Robert was in white flannels and the girl in a white tennis slip that was obviously inspired by Wimbledon but owed not a little to the art of home dressmaking.

'Gosh!' said William. 'He's with that awful Roxana Lytton.'

'Well, he ought to be in a good temper, then,' said Ginger. 'He's bats on her, isn't he?'

'Yes, but she's not bats on him now. She used to be, but she's met someone called Osbert an' she's bats on him now instead.'

It was clear that all was not well with the couple. Roxana's perfect mouth was set in lines of petulance, and Robert's countenance was overcast.

William hesitated.

'P'r'aps I'd better not—' he began.

'Oh, go on,' said Ginger. 'Have a shot at it anyway.'

Impelled by his friend, William stumbled into the track of the approaching couple.

'What on *earth*—?' said Robert, pulling himself up and directing an angry gaze at his young brother.

'What do you mean by barging into us like that? Have you no manners? Have you no—'

'Listen, Robert,' interrupted William desperately. 'It's only two bob an' it's wizard an' if it isn't a Gloster Meteor it's jolly like one . . . An' listen, Robert. I'll do everything you want me to all the rest of my life if you'll—'

'Get out of the way,' said Robert wrathfully, 'or I'll—'

William hastily removed himself from the path of the couple and they passed down the road.

Roxana's petulant voice floated back to them.

'It's so *maddening*. Daddy's done everything he could and she won't even *listen*. It isn't as if she wanted the ground.'

'What's she talkin' about?' said Ginger.

'Oh, I remember now,' said William vaguely. 'I heard Robert talkin' about it at home. They want to make a tennis-court – Roxana's family does – an' they want to buy that bit of land at the bottom of the Botts' orchard that sticks out into their garden an' Mrs Bott won't sell it to them.'

'Gosh! The things they find to make a fuss about!' said Ginger in a tone of mystification. 'It's a rotten game, tennis, anyway. Jus' hittin' a ball over a net. You can't even get a goal in it.'

William was gazing back at Robert and Roxana.

'I 'spect she's goin' on an' on' an' on at him,' he said. 'Well, it serves him right for not givin' us that two bob.'

William was right. Roxana was going on and on and on, and Robert's face grew each moment more harassed and troubled.

'It's so *mean* of her. Daddy's written and telephoned and been to see her and she just gets ruder and ruder. He wanted to have the tennis-court ready for my twenty-first birthday and it's just awful of her not to let us have it. He doesn't mind what he pays but she just won't sell it. She's – well, I won't soil my tongue with what she is.'

'I'm terribly sorry,' said Robert.

Roxana gave her golden head an angry toss.

'That's what everyone says but no one *does* anything.'

'There doesn't seem anything one can do,' said Robert.

'Oh, yes,' said Roxana sarcastically. 'That's what everyone says, too. When I think of the number of friends I thought I had, who said they'd do anything for me – *anything* – and the way that, now I'm in desperate trouble and need help, they all leave me in the lurch' – she sighed – 'except Osbert.'

'Osbert?' challenged Robert aggressively. 'What can Osbert do?'

It was Osbert – a dim youth with a man-of-the-world manner and a car of excessively contemporary design – who had ousted Robert from his position as Roxana's favoured suitor. She gave him the special smile that she had once kept for Robert. She went for drives with him. She asked him to tea. She held with him those long confidential discussions about nothing in particular that she used to hold with Robert. And Robert, expelled from his paradise, could only watch and gnash his teeth.

'He hasn't decided yet,' said Roxana with dignity, 'but he's thinking out a plan, which is more than you're doing.'

Robert began a snort of amused contempt, then checked it

midway and decided to make a last desperate effort to re-establish the old relations with the beloved.

'Don't worry, Roxana,' he said tenderly. 'I expect it will sort itself out. Things do sort themselves out. I've been in lots of jams myself and they've generally – well, sorted themselves out . . . Listen, Roxana, there's a new roadhouse just beyond that village that you liked when we went through it last month. You said it would look sweet done in colours on a Christmas calendar, you remember. It wouldn't have occurred to me because I'm not artistic like you, but I felt it was a beautiful thought . . . Well, I wondered if you'd care to go out there on my motor-bike next Saturday and have tea there . . . '

'I'm sorry,' said Roxana distantly. 'I'm going out with Osbert in his car next Saturday.'

'Oh . . . ' said Robert. 'Well, you won't forget that you're going to the tennis club dance with me, will you?'

Roxana raised delicate eyebrows.

'The tennis club dance?' she said. 'I'm sorry, Robert. You must have misunderstood me. I've arranged to go to that with Osbert.'

'Osbert!' groaned Robert.

'Well, you see, Robert,' said Roxana sweetly, 'Osbert's the only one of my friends who's standing by me in this dreadful crisis. As I told you, he's thinking out a plan. He doesn't just – throw me aside like an old glove as the rest of you do.'

'If there's anything Osbert Sanderstead can do,' said Robert savagely, 'I can do it. And I'll *do* it, too. I won't just talk about it like that braying jackass.'

Roxana drew herself up.

'How dare you speak of my friends like that, Robert!' she said. 'I don't wish to hear another word from you. I—' Curiosity got the better of her indignation. 'What could you do, anyway?'

'I could go to that Bott woman,' said Robert impulsively,

'and tell her what I think of her . . . and I *will* go to her, too. I – I'll insist that she lets you have the ground. She needs a *man* to deal with her. I – I won't let her get away with it. Once she has me to deal with, she'll – she'll change her tune.'

Roxana stared at him, half impressed, half incredulous.

'Well, Daddy's been at her over and over again. I don't know what you've got that Daddy hasn't.'

Robert tried to think of something he'd got that Daddy hadn't and finally gave up the attempt. Incredulity was beginning to possess him, too, and the spurt of resentment that had prompted his rash offer was dying down. Mrs Bott was a formidable opponent. Few people joined issue with her and came away victorious.

'You're going to her now, are you?' said Roxana, torn between hope and despair.

'I don't know about this very moment,' said Robert with a mirthless smile. They had reached the lane that led to Roxana's house. 'I'll – I'll just see you home first.'

'No, don't trouble to do that, Robert. Osbert's coming to tea and he'll probably be there waiting for me. You'd better go straight on to Mrs Bott's, hadn't you?'

'Well – er – yes,' said Robert, giving a hunted glance around. 'Yes, I suppose I had. She – she may be out of course.'

'You can wait till she comes in, can't you? . . . Well, I must hurry on now. I don't want to keep Osbert waiting. Good-bye.'

'Good-bye,' said Robert in a hollow voice.

He stood hesitating for a moment or two, then adjusted his collar and with set stern face started off in the direction of the Hall. He walked slowly up the drive, stopping occasionally as if to admire the nondescript clumps of shrubs that bordered it. Reaching the front door, he drew a deep breath then raised the knocker and let it fall lightly back in a way that, with luck, might fail to attract the attention of the inmates. A housemaid came to the door. He assumed an air of hauteur.

'I wish to speak to Mrs Bott,' he said. 'Urgently. On private business.'

The housemaid vanished, and, after a short interval, re-appeared.

'Mrs Bott will see you in the morning-room,' she said, with a hauteur that almost equalled Robert's.

Robert went into the morning-room.

He emerged some moments later with a heightened colour and made his way hastily down the drive, throwing an occasional glance over his shoulder as if fearful of pursuit.

The interview had been a short one and in the course of it Mrs Bott had disposed of him with a few brief trenchant words. She had called him an interfering jackanapes, an impudent puppy, a nincompoop and, for no particular reason, a two-faced snake in the grass. She had said that she wouldn't sell that bit of land now for all the tea in China and had added that she'd put the police on him if he as much as showed his nose inside her house again. She had ended the interview by advancing upon him with so threatening an aspect that he had turned and fled from her in ignominious panic.

She stood now at the morning-room window, watching his departure. She was still breathing heavily, but there was a faint look of satisfaction on her plump little face. It had been a relief to unload on Robert some of the resentment that she felt against life in general. For Mrs Bott, like Robert, was labouring under a sense of grievance . . .

Ever since her husband had invented a sauce whose sales had raised her from the wife of a small grocer to the mistress of the Hall she had longed to get among what she called the 'high-ups', but the high-ups ignored her overtures with a bland politeness that baffled her at every turn. There were times when she accepted this state of things. There were times when she rebelled against it and returned to the fray.

She had lately returned to the fray. Hearing that on the committee of the Women's Guild there were – in addition to the Honourable Mrs Everton-Massinger, the secretary – three ladies of title and the mother-in-law of a bishop, she had joined the Guild, contributed lavishly to its funds, provided magnificent teas for all its meetings . . . and still, after two months' intensive effort, had not been asked to sit on the committee. It was, she was beginning to feel, more than flesh and blood could stand, and Robert, proffering his ill-timed request, had borne the full brunt of her anger.

Her plump little face a deep purple colour, she made her way to the library – a spacious book-lined room where Mr Bott rested after meals and did his football pools.

'That there Robert Brown,' she burst out stormily as she entered, 'pokin' his nose into that there bit o' land at the bottom of the orchard! What's it got to do with 'im, anyway? *H*im.' Mrs Bott was apt to drop her aitches but generally managed to pick them up again before they had gone too far. 'That there bit o' land belongs to us an' we're not selling it, not to no one, an' I told the saucy young 'ound so straight. *H*ound.'

Mr Bott looked up from his football pools.

'We could easy let it go, love,' he said mildly.

'Not while I'm alive, we won't,' said Mrs Bott with an ominous ring to her voice. 'If they think they can treat me like dirt, buying land off us whenever they've a mind to, they've got to think again. *Use* me, that's what they do. Make a mug of me. Same as that there Women's Guild. I'm good enough to give 'em tea and find money for 'em, but ham I good enough to go on their committees an' suchlike? Ho, no!'

Mr Bott gazed sadly at the podgy little figure of his wife. He did not share her passion for high life, but he was deeply attached to her and suffered with her in all her disappointments.

'In the swim, that's what you've got to be to get in with 'em,' she said, her voice sinking to a doleful note, 'an' I don't seem to be able to get in the swim no'ow, 'owever 'ard I try. *H*ard.'

'You do your best, love,' said Mr Bott soothingly.

'Flower arrangements an' budgerigars,' said Mrs Bott. 'That's what they're all goin' for now. They go to classes in Flower Arrangements an' they've got budgerigars what talk and if you don't do none of them there things you're not in the swim.'

'Well, you've been to a Flower Arrangement class,' said Mr Bott.

Mrs Bott was silent, thinking of the hour she had spent at a Flower Arrangement class, when such words as Design, Balance, Scale, Symbolism, Focal Interest, Rhythm, Fillers and Dominants had floated meaninglessly over her bewildered head.

'Yes, but I couldn't make 'ead nor tail of it, Botty,' she said at last. '*H*ead. I can do a nice vase of sweet-peas an' Gypsophila as good as anyone. Proper dainty, they look, but they don't seem to want 'em dainty no longer. I sent one in to their competition an' they didn't as much as look at it.'

Mr Bott sought for some crumb of comfort to offer her.

'Well, you got a budgerigar, love.'

'Yes, but it won't talk, Botty,' wailed his wife. 'Theirs talk. They say "Polly, put the kettle on," an' "Ta-ra-ra-ra-boom-de-ay," an' "Good old Winny" an' things like that.'

'Well, you've got to 'ave patience, love. You've only 'ad it a week.'

'Yes, but I've been on an' on at it with "Pop Goes the Weasel" day in day out ever since it came an' it won't say a word. Jus' sits an' looks down its nose at me same as all the rest of 'em.'

She sighed, then a faint ray of consolation seemed to shine through her despondency.

'Anyway, I've took the stuffing out of that there Robert Brown,' she said.

She had certainly taken the stuffing out of Robert. He was standing in the garden, hands in pockets, gaze bent gloomily on the ground. He had failed in his mission. He had lost Roxana. The obnoxious Osbert had probably by now devised some cunning plan by which he could lay the fateful piece of land at Roxana's feet and win her lasting gratitude. There was, Robert felt, nothing left in his life worth living for. It was just as he had reached this conclusion that William appeared at the garden gate. He had paid the toy shop another visit and made the shopman a sporting offer to weed his garden, polish his car, clean his windows and wash down his front doorstep in exchange for the aeroplane – only to be summarily ejected from the shop before he had had time to add the further offer, which had just occurred to him, of cleaning his chimneys.

He watched Robert's sagging figure for a few moments; then, on an impulse and feeling that, after all, he had nothing to lose, decided to approach him again. He approached him warily, keeping at a safe distance, poised ready for flight.

'I say, Robert!' he said. 'If you could jus' let me have two bob . . . '

Robert turned a lack-lustre eye on him. His mind was still so busy plumbing the depths of despair that he didn't take in the full meaning of what was happening. Someone was demanding two bob from him. Absently he brought out half a crown from his pocket and placed it in the grubby outstretched palm.

'Gosh!' said William faintly. '*Gosh*, Robert! Thanks awfully. I'll give you the change when I've got it.'

'Keep the change,' said Robert wearily.

What did wealth matter, what did anything matter, now that he had lost Roxana and his life was blighted for ever?

William walked away in a sort of dream. He couldn't

believe it. Nothing like this had ever happened to him before. So deeply was he impressed by it that his sense of gratitude to Robert drove out every other emotion. He didn't even want to go and buy the aeroplane. He only wanted to relieve his mind of its burden of obligation. Robert was plainly in trouble and the source of the trouble was, William knew, the piece of land at the bottom of Mrs Bott's orchard. William, an inveterate trespasser on other people's property, was familiar with the piece of land. It was a sort of promontory, jutting out into the garden of Roxana's father, that no one had ever bothered to cultivate, that was not indeed worth cultivating. Weeds flourished in it shoulder-high. Bindweed romped blithely from end to end of it. Thistles raised their heads in it exultantly. Seedlings from the neighbouring trees made miniature forests in it. He and Ginger had once tried to play Cowboys and Indians in it and had had to give up the attempt.

It was outrageous, thought William, that Robert's peace of mind should be shattered by a bit of ground that you couldn't even play Cowboys and Indians in. He must do something about it. He – the idea came to him quite suddenly – he would go to Mrs Bott and reason with her. He would put Robert's case before her and plead the justice of his cause. His memory of previous interviews with Mrs Bott was not encouraging, but William's optimism was proof against discouraging memories. He would do it at once.

Arriving breathless and panting at the front door of the Hall, he put all the pent-up force of his resolution into his attack on the large iron knocker.

The housemaid who answered his knock fixed him with a coldly disparaging eye.

'D'you want to break the door down?' she said.

'No,' replied William. 'I want to speak to Mrs Bott. It's somethin' very important what can't wait.'

'Another of 'em,' said the housemaid with a shrug.

She assumed her air of hauteur. 'What name shall I say?'

William eyed her suspiciously.

'It's William Brown, if you don't know,' he said, 'an' I bet you do.'

'I'd be deaf and blind in this here village if I didn't,' agreed the housemaid as she vanished into the recesses of the stately hall.

'She'll see you in the morning-room,' she said when she returned, 'and wipe your shoes and pull up your socks and tidy yourself up a bit and try to look a bit less like something out of a loony bin.'

'All right, all right, all right,' said William. 'You should know what they look like.' He performed a hasty toilet by running his fingers through his hair and wiping his face with something that passed for a handkerchief. 'Will I do now?'

'You'd *do* for anyone.' She took him by the ear and led him across the hall to a closed door. Then opening the door and dropping her left eyelid at William she announced resonantly:

'Master William Brown.'

Mrs Bott, standing by the chimney piece, received her visitor with an icy stare.

'Well?' she said. 'What d'you want?'

William paused for a moment, then plunged headlong into his recital.

'It's only two bob,' he said, 'an' I bet it's a Gloster Meteor an' Robert gave me two an' six an' they want the tennis-court for her twenty-first birthday an' he said keep the change an' you wouldn't miss it an' no one's ever let me keep the change before an' you've got a great huge garden without it an' I feel jolly grateful 'cause we hadn't any money at all an' now we can buy monster humbugs as well as the aeroplane an'—' He paused for breath.

'What are you talking about?' said Mrs Bott tersely.

'That bit of land that Roxana's father wants to buy off you.'

'YOU CAN KEEP YOUR FINGER OUT OF THIS PIE, WILLIAM
BROWN,' SAID MRS BOTT. 'SO CLEAR OUT.'

Mrs Bott looked at him for a moment in silence. She was still purple-faced and breathing heavily, but she had brunted the edge of her indignation in the interview with Robert. Her spirit was not broken, but it was showing signs of strain. Although she was as determined as ever not to sell the piece of land, she was beginning to search for reasons to justify her attitude.

'They ought to be ashamed of themselves, using a child like you,' she temporised.

'They're not usin' me,' said William. 'They don't know I've come. And' – indignantly – 'I'm not a child. Gosh! I shall be twelve next birthday.'

'Now listen to me, William Brown,' said Mrs Bott. 'That there bit of land's no use for nothin' – not for a tennis-court nor nothin' else. It didn't seem to fit in with the orchard, so we left it an' there it's been year after year, full of weeds. *Cluttered* with weeds, it is. You couldn't get them there weeds out, not with a bulldozer, you couldn't. So you can just keep your finger out of this pie, William Brown, an' I don't know what I'm doin' wastin' my time on a whippersnapper like you. So clear out.'

Her fighting spirit had returned. The light of battle gleamed in her eye. William cleared out.

But he was not a boy to abandon a project at the first set-back. His brow was drawn into a thoughtful frown as he walked down the drive. She had said that she wouldn't sell the land because it was full of weeds. The remedy was simple. He would clear it of weeds. He would clear it of weeds and then she wouldn't have a leg to stand on. She'd *have* to sell it to Roxana's father if he cleared it of weeds. A mental vision of the almost impenetrable jungle damped his ardour for a moment but only for a moment. He would get Ginger to help him. Together they would make short work of it. He would fetch Ginger now and—

He had reached the gate and, glancing down the road, he saw Ginger walking towards him, carrying his aunt's cat. It was an ancient somnolent cat of rusty black that allowed itself to be carried anywhere by anyone without interest or protest. It generally spent the day sleeping in Ginger's aunt's armchair, awakening only to partake of the large and appetising meals that Ginger's aunt prepared for it at regular intervals.

'I've taken it to the vet,' said Ginger, 'an' its ear's all right an' she's not goin' to give me a tip for takin' it. I knew she wouldn't.'

'Well, come on quick,' said William. 'Never mind the ole cat. Robert's given me half a crown so we've got to weed that bit of land at the bottom of Mrs Bott's orchard so's she'll sell it to Roxana's father. We'll soon pull 'em up an' we'll get some monster humbugs as well as the aeroplane.'

Ginger considered this with a perplexed frown.

'I'd better take the cat back to my aunt's first,' he said.

'No, we can't wait for you to do that,' said William impatiently. 'We've got to clear those weeds out quick. Bring the ole cat along with you. It won't run away. It never does.'

'All right,' said Ginger, following William to the weed-infested piece of ground at the bottom of the orchard.

'Gosh! There's a lot of them,' he said, peering about him through a tangle of thistle and willow-herb.

'They pull up easy,' William assured him, dragging a handful up by the roots. 'We'll just go on pulling an' pullin' till there's none left, then she'll *have* to sell it.'

They worked in silence for some moments, then Ginger spoke in a quick warning voice.

'I say, William. Look! There's a gard'ner over there cutting the hedge an' he's seen us.'

The gardener had certainly seen them. He was staring at them grimly, menacingly. Then, with an air of purpose, he laid down his shears and began slowly to make his way towards them.

'Come on quick!' said William.

Flight to the road was barred by the gardener's advancing figure. The only way left open to them was through the orchard towards the garden and house.

'Hi!' shouted the gardener, speeding his slow steps to a run.

'He's comin' after us,' panted Ginger.

'Hi!' shouted the gardener again, beginning to run still faster.

They fled through the orchard to the lawn and dodged behind one of the herbaceous borders. William still clutched his handful of weeds. Ginger had discarded his weeds but still carried the large black cat, who remained unmoved and unperturbed by the adventure.

'Quick! Into the shrub'ry!' panted William.

They plunged into the shrubbery. The gardener plunged after them. They dodged round the shrubs. The gardener dodged after them. A small lawn separated the shrubbery from an open french window of the house.

'Come on! Quick!' gasped William and, followed by Ginger, darted across the plot of grass through the open window and into Mrs Bott's drawing-room.

The room was empty except for the budgerigar, who drooped in his cage on a small mahogany cupboard near the fireplace.

William and Ginger looked out of the window from the cover of the curtains. The gardener was still searching the shrubbery.

'Well, we've thrown him off all right,' said William. 'We'll jus' wait here till he's tired of looking for us an' then we'll—'

He stopped. The sound of Mrs Bott's voice and another voice sounded in the distance . . . growing nearer . . . nearer . . . It was clear that Mrs Bott was bringing a visitor across the hall towards the drawing-room. William threw a desperate glance out of the window. The gardener had left the shrubbery and was standing in the middle of the plot of grass, gazing suspiciously at the house. The voices of Mrs Bott and her visitor were almost at the door. There appeared to him to be no means of escape . . . till his eyes lit on a vast tallboy that stood against the wall.

'We could jus' squeeze behind that,' he said.

'Not with this cat, I couldn't,' said Ginger, 'and not with those weeds, you couldn't.'

'Well, let's bung them anywhere,' said William. 'I bet she won't notice.'

His glance shot round the room again. On a table by the window was a large empty ornamental plant-pot. He thrust his handful of weeds into it, snatched the cat from Ginger's arms, opened the cupboard beneath the budgerigar's cage, flung the cat inside and, followed by Ginger, scraped his solid person painfully between the tallboy and the wall. They were only just in time. The moment the last of their persons had disappeared from view, the door opened and Mrs Bott entered, accompanied by the Honourable Mrs Everton-Massinger.

* * *

WILLIAM FLUNG THE CAT INSIDE THE CUPBOARD.

Mrs Bott was in the library with her husband, recovering from her interview with William, when she saw the Honourable Mrs Everton-Massinger coming up the drive.

'I bet she's coming to ask for something, Botty,' she said dismally. 'It's all they ever does – ask me for things.'

And the prophecy proved correct.

Mrs Everton-Massinger was tall and thin with small tight features and an air of bright intensity. Her shabby tweeds held a vague suggestion of county and the rest of her more than a vague suggestion of art-and-craftiness, committee meetings and the platforms of village halls.

She greeted Mr and Mrs Bott, threw a pained glance at Mr

Bott's football pools form, and came at once to the purpose of her visit.

'I wonder if you'd be so good as to help us out again, Mrs Bott,' she said in her nasal high-pitched voice. 'We're having a joint garden meeting with the Hadley Women's Guild next month. A pity it falls in the month when Lady Barnham will be away but it's just one of those things . . .'

'Yes,' said Mrs Bott.

She tried to sound cold and dignified but she could only sound wistful and dejected.

'We wondered whether you'd be so good as to see to the tea again. The Young Wives would have helped us, but they're having an outing to Margate that day. Such a pity, but – well, it's just one of those things.'

'Yes,' said Mrs Bott again.

'So, if we may count on you . . .'

'Yes, I'll see to it,' said Mrs Bott with a touch of bitterness in her voice. 'I generally does, don't I?'

'So good of you,' said Mrs Everton-Massinger with mechanical graciousness. 'I'm not sure what we shall do if it's wet.'

A light sprang suddenly into Mrs Bott's face.

'You could 'ave it in my drawing-room,' she said eagerly. 'P'raps you'd like to come and see my drawing-room. I've just had all the chairs re-up'olstered. It looks a treat. *H*olstered.'

'Well . . .' said Mrs Everton-Massinger without enthusiasm.

She evidently had no consuming desire to see Mrs Bott's drawing-room. But Mrs Bott had a consuming desire to show it to her.

'This way,' she said.

Mr Bott raised his eyes from his football pools form, his pencil poised over Arsenal, and sighed as his wife and her visitor left the room.

Their progress to the drawing-room was slow. Mrs Bott had

to stop at the window and point out the extensiveness of the grounds, had to stop at the magnificent hall wardrobe and display its elaborate fittings, had to stop at a large gilt-framed oil-painting and explain, 'It's a real old master. 'Olbein or Landseer, I forget which. I get a bit muddled. *H*olbein. Cost Botty a pretty penny, anyway.'

The visitor's manner became more and more distant and depression settled again over Mrs Bott's spirit.

'An' this 'ere 's the drawing-room,' she said, throwing open the door.

Mrs Everton-Massinger glanced coldly round the large ornate over-furnished room.

'Not at all suitable for our little gathering, I'm afraid,' she said.

Then her eyes lit on the weeds that William had thrust into the plant-pot and a gleam came into them.

'Oh, Mrs Bott!' she said. 'What a wonderful Arrangement!'

Mrs Bott gaped but Mrs Everton-Massinger had crossed the room to the plant-pot and was examining it, her hands clasped, her whole thin body quivering with ecstasy.

'The *composition!* . . . The *line* of that groundsel and yarrow! . . . The *rhythm* of the nettles and willow-herb! It's wonderful! *Wonderful!* . . . That seeded hemlock in the middle is an inspiration . . . And that ragwort to complete the balance! Wonderful! . . . And— Oh, Mrs Bott! The marvellous touch of *symbolism* in putting that seeded foxglove close to the one in bloom! And – oh, those thistles are so just right to give the sweep, the range, the compass. Oh, the originality, the *rightness* of the whole thing!'

Mrs Bott had grown pale. She was opening and closing her mouth with fish-like motions. But at that moment a sleepy 'miaow' sounded from the direction of the budgerigar's cage.

The visitor swung round.

'Your budgie! . . . But, Mrs Bott, what a *marvellous* cat imitation!'

Again a sleepy 'miaow' came from – as it seemed – the budgerigar's cage.

'How *did* you teach it to miaow like that, Mrs Bott? It might be a real cat! How long have you had it?'

'About a week,' said Mrs Bott, rallying her scattered forces.

'Could it speak at all when you got it?'

'No,' said Mrs Bott.

'And you've taught it to miaow like that in this short time?' said Mrs Everton-Massinger. Her voice became more nasal and high-pitched than ever. 'Oh, it's marvellous.' Another 'miaow' sounded, still sleepy but on a rising note of protest. '*Marvellous!* I've worked on mine for months and even now it can only say "Rule Britannia," and so indistinctly that several of my friends say they don't recognise the words at all. This wonderful cat imitation in less than a week . . . ' She sighed and shrugged. 'Oh, well, it's just one of those things . . . '

She looked at the plant-pot, the budgerigar's cage and then at Mrs Bott. There was a new respect in her eyes, a note almost of humility in her voice as she went on:

'I wonder if you'd consider coming on to the committee, Mrs Bott. There happens to be a vacancy and if I propose you and Lady Barnham seconds you – as I'm quite sure she will – there'll be no doubt at all of your election.'

Mrs Bott gaped, blinked, gulped and gasped.

'Oo, thank you,' she said. 'Thank you ever so.'

'And now I'm afraid I must be going,' said Mrs Everton-Massinger.

Still gaping, blinking, gulping, gasping, Mrs Bott led her visitor from the room.

As soon as the door had closed on them, the two boys crept

'BUT, MRS BOTT,' SAID THE VISITOR, SWINGING ROUND,
'WHAT A MARVELLOUS CAT IMITATION!'

out from behind the tallboy, dragged the sleepily protesting
cat from the cupboard and made their way through the french
windows across the now unguarded lawn, down the drive to
the gate. Mrs Everton-Massinger passed them at the gate. Her
thin face wore a look of surprise and bewilderment.

'They talked a lot of nonsense, didn't they?' said Ginger as
they stood watching the departing figure. 'I couldn't make out
what they were talkin' about, could you?'

'No, I couldn't hear what they said anyway,' said William. 'My ears were all squashed up between the wall and that big chest of drawers thing . . . Anyway, we can't do any more weedin' now. That ole gardener'll be on the lookout for us. Let's take the cat to your aunt's an' then go an' buy the aeroplane.'

'Yes, let's,' said Ginger. 'I say, we were jolly lucky ole Mrs Bott didn't find us in that room. I thought that cat'd given us away once, didn't you?'

'Yes . . . She'd have half-murdered us if she'd found us,' said William. 'She's in an awful temper today.'

But Mrs Bott was not in an awful temper. She was standing beside her husband, gazing down at him, a blissful smile on her plump little face.

'I'm *on*, Botty,' she was saying triumphantly. 'I'm on that there committee at last.'

'I'm glad, love,' said Mr Bott, folding up his football pools form and putting it into an envelope. 'What made 'em put you on?'

'The drawing-room . . . Flowers in a vase an' that there budgerigar startin' to talk. It said "Miaow" plain as plain.'

'Well I never!' said Mr Bott. 'Thought you was tryin' to teach it "Pop Goes the Weasel."'

'Yes, I was, but it started off on "miaow" all of its own accord . . . An', Botty I feel that happy, I want to make someone else 'appy too. *H*appy. I'll let 'em have that piece of ground. I'm not goin' to ring up that Lytton man after all the things he's said to me. I'll ring up Robert Brown an' he can tell 'em.'

'That's a good idea, love,' said Mr Bott, affixing a stamp to his football pools form envelope. 'He'll be grateful.'

'He was grateful all right,' said Mrs Bott when she returned from her telephone conversation with Robert, 'but he seemed in a bit of a hurry.'

Robert was now engaged in telephoning Roxana, beaming ecstatically into the instrument.

'I've been to see Mrs Bott, Roxana darling,' he was saying, 'and she's willing to let you have that piece of ground.'

'Oh, *Robert*!' gasped Roxana. 'How did you manage it?'

'Oh, I – er – I just put it to her,' said Robert nonchalantly. 'I just put your point of view to her. I – well, I made her see reason in the end. She didn't decide on the spot. She took a little time to think it over, but she's just rung me up to say that she's thought it over and that she'll agree to it.'

'Oh, Robert, you're wonderful,' said the dulcet voice at the other end of the wire. 'Simply wonderful! And all the time you were *acting* that wretched Osbert was just dithering. I've *taxed* him with it, Robert, and he had to admit that he hadn't got a plan at all. He hadn't even started thinking one out. I was furious . . . Robert, I'd love to go with you to that roadhouse place on Saturday . . . and, Robert, it's all right about the tennis club dance.'

'Oh, Roxana!' said Robert. 'May I – may I come over and see you?'

'Yes, *do*, Robert. I've sent Osbert away. I couldn't stand him a moment longer.'

Hurrying out of the gate, his mind busy with a hasty reconstruction of his interview with Mrs Bott, he collided with William and Ginger. Their cheeks bulged with monster humbugs and their heads were bent over a small toy aeroplane that their imaginations had already transformed into the star turn of a Farnborough display.

'Oh, take yourselves and your wretched contraption out of the way,' said Robert impatiently.

The mellowness that misfortune had shed over his spirit had vanished. It had regained its usual toughness.

'Gosh!' said William, picking up the happily uninjured aeroplane and turning to watch his brother's hurried progress down the road. 'Everyone seems mad today. Robert's mad an' Mrs Bott was mad . . . ' He looked at the chimneys of the Hall that could be seen over the trees and chuckled. 'I bet she's madder than ever if she's found those weeds in that pot. She mus' have found 'em by now, too. I'd like to hear what she's sayin'.'

'It won't do it no more, Botty,' Mrs Bott was saying in a tone of mystification. 'Did it as plain as plain when she was there an' now it jus' won't do it.'

'Well, it can't go on miaowing all day, love,' said Mr Bott. 'It's got to have a bit of a rest sometimes. I shouldn't worry about it.'

'I'm not worrying about it, Botty, but' – a thoughtful look came into her face – 'there was somethin' a bit *queer* about the whole thing.'

'Ow d'you mean, queer?' said her husband.

'Well, you know, I don't remember *doin'* that there flower arrangement at all. Not a single blessed mem'ry of it, I 'aven't got. I *must* 'ave done it 'cause there it was, plain as the nose on your face. *H*ave. I must 'ave done it in a sort of trance.'

'Yes, you might 'ave,' agreed Mr Bott.

'Or' – with vague memories of a lecture on psychology that she had once attended in the Village Hall – 'me subconscious may 'ave done it, Botty, without me knowin' anything about it.'

'It might 'ave,' agreed Mr Bott.

The thoughtful look had deepened on Mrs Bott's face.

'An' there's somethin' else that's queer about it, too, Botty.'

'Yes?' said Mr Bott.

'You know that tallboy in the drawing-room?'

'Yes, love?'

'Well, you know it's got four legs, two at each end . . . Well, I got a sort of idea this afternoon that it had eight.'

'*Eight?*' said Mr Bott, startled.

'Yes. Two at each end and four in the middle against the wall. Mind you, I never looked at it *straight*. I was that took up by what she was saying that I only sort of saw it out of the corner of my eye, so to speak, but I've got a sort of mem'ry of it standing there with eight legs.'

'Not eight,' said Mr Bott firmly. He could swallow the trance and the subconscious, but he couldn't swallow the tallboy with eight legs. 'Not eight, it couldn't have had. Not the tallboy. You must have been mistook.'

'I expect I was,' said Mrs Bott. 'Oh, well—' She sighed and her voice unconsciously took on a high-pitched nasal accent as she continued, 'I suppose it's just one of them there things.'

'That's it, love,' said Mr Bott reassuringly. 'It's just one o' them there things.'

Chapter 5

William Gets a Scoop

'Let's do somethin' we've not done for a long time,' said Ginger.

The Outlaws were sitting in a circle on the floor in William's bedroom. A shower had driven them from the garden, where they had been playing Cowboys and Indians, and now, though the shower was over, they felt reluctant to continue the game, which had begun to pall even before the rain started.

Jumble lay in the centre of the circle, his head on his paws, his eyes closed, as if even he were affected by the atmosphere of boredom.

'There isn't anythin' we've not done for a long time,' said Douglas.

'There must be,' said Henry. 'Think of all the days there are in a year an' we do somethin' diff'rent on nearly all of 'em.'

'Tell you what!' said William. 'Let's do a newspaper. It's a jolly long time since we did a newspaper.'

Jumble sat up and thumped his tail on the floor in approval, and the others looked at William with interest.

'Y-yes,' said Ginger. 'It's not a bad idea.'

'The las' time we did it, there was some sort of a muddle,' said Douglas.

'It was Violet Elizabeth,' said William. 'She messed it up – I forget jus' how – but we'll jolly well keep her out of it this time.'

'Yes, we jolly well will,' agreed the others and Jumble again thumped his tail on the floor in approval.

'What'll we have?' said Ginger. 'In the newspaper, I mean.'

'They have news in newspapers,' said Henry simply.

'Well, there isn't any news,' said Ginger. 'My father's always sayin' there isn't any news. Whenever my mother asks him at breakfast what news there is in his newspaper he always says there isn't any.'

'Well, we can invent news, can't we?' said William. 'I bet that's what real ones do, invent it if there isn't any . . . '

'It's goin' to be jolly diff'cult inventin' news,' said Douglas, 'an' there's lors against it. My aunt once knew someone that was had up by the p'lice for saying somethin' about someone else that wasn't true. It frightened her so much she got an awful disease called jaundice an' turned yellow all over.'

'That's right,' said William. 'Start makin' objections. Soon as ever I get a good idea you all start makin' objections. How d'you think real newspapers'd get done if everyone that was s'posed to be doin' 'em sat around makin' objections about there not bein' any news an' their aunts turnin' yellow all over?'

'It wasn't my aunt that turned yellow,' said Douglas. 'It—'

'Oh, shut up about your aunt,' said William. 'I jolly well don't care what colour your aunt turned. Now let's get on with this newspaper.'

'Real newspapers try 'n' get news that other newspapers haven't got,' said Henry. 'They call it a scoop.'

'We'll have one of 'em, then,' said William casually. 'We'll fix that up later . . . What do they have besides news an' scoops?'

'They have advertisements,' said Henry.

'That's easy,' said William. 'You jus' draw pictures of people drinkin' things an' eatin' things an' wearing hats an' things an' tell other people to buy 'em. I bet the editor draws the pictures. I'll be him.'

'An' there's got to be a sub-editor,' said Henry.

'I'll be him,' said Ginger.

'An' I've thought of somethin' else,' said William. 'I'll have an Animals' Corner an' write about animals in it.'

'An' there's got to be a po'm in a newspaper,' said Henry. 'A po'm about spring.'

'It needn't be about spring,' said William. 'Po'ms about spring are soppy.'

'All po'ms are soppy,' said Douglas.

'No, they're not,' said William. 'There's po'ms about adventures. There's one about a man who kept a bridge in the brave days of old.'

'What did he keep a bridge for,' said Douglas.

'I've forgot,' said William. 'I 'spect it was jus' one of the things they kept in the brave days of old. Things weren't as excitin' then as what they are now. No one'd thought of goin' to the moon, same as I'm goin' to. Anyway it wasn't a bad po'm 'cept it was too long.'

'All po'ms are too long,' said Ginger. 'There ought to be a lor that they can't be more than one verse.'

'An' about spring,' said Henry.

'About adventure,' said William.

'There ought to be po'ms about things to eat,' said Douglas. 'I don't know why people don't write po'ms about raspb'ry jellies an' ice-cream an' doughnuts an' trifle an' liqu'rice bootlaces an' things like that. They're a jolly sight more excitin' than spring an' keepin' bridges.'

'Love,' said Ginger. 'Po'ms ought to be about love. All great po'ts wrote po'ms about love. Shakespeare did an' so does that woman called Heartsease that writes po'ms in the *Hadley Times*. There ought to be a po'm about love.'

'Well, there's not goin' to be,' said William firmly. 'There's only goin' to be one po'm an' it's goin' to be about adventure.'

'Spring,' said Henry.

'Food,' said Douglas.

'Love,' persisted Ginger.

'Spring! Food! Love!' jeered William. 'You're jus' a lot of cissies.'

'Who's a cissie?' said Ginger scrambling to his feet.

'You are,' said William, the urge of battle rising in him.

'Say it again!' said Ginger.

'Cissie!' said William happily.

The resultant scuffle began as a fight between William and Ginger and ended as an All against All wrestling match, with the four of them rolling about the floor on top of each other and Jumble joining in as best he could. They only stopped because each combatant was so firmly pinioned by an antagonist that he could not move and because they were too helpless with laughter to continue.

'What are you doing, boys?' called Mrs Brown from downstairs when the contest was at its height.

'Nothin',' answered William reassuringly.

'Well, do try to make less noise about it,' said Mrs Brown.

They disentangled themselves and sat panting on the floor.

'It was a draw,' pronounced William, 'so we'll have a po'm about spring *an*' food *an*' love *an*' adventure an' write a line each.'

'Jolly good idea!' said the others, exhilarated by the fight, which had dispelled the last vestige of their boredom and only done such minor pieces of damage as breaking a leg of William's bedroom chair – an article of furniture broken at such frequent intervals that it had long ceased to be regarded as an article of furniture – and pulling part of the window curtain loose from its moorings.

'My foot feels funny,' said Ginger. 'I think it's gone to sleep.'

'Put it to bed, then,' said Douglas, and the others shouted with mirth at his wit.

But Ginger, walking to the window to awake the sleeping member, had caught sight of a well-known figure entering the garden gate.

'I say, William,' he said, 'here's Miss Milton comin' to your house.'

'Gosh!' said William, his mind moving quickly over the events of the last few days. 'Well, I can't think of anythin' I've done, 'cept Jumble chasin' her ole cat. P'r'aps she thought I set him on to it.'

'P'raps you did,' said Ginger.

'Well, I may've sort of said, "Cats, Jumble!" jus' to myself, but how should I know he'd hear an' start chasin' it?'

'You ought to by now,' said Henry.

'If she's come to complain about that, they'll come up an' stop the newspaper,' said Douglas anxiously. 'Let's clear off quick.'

'Yes, let's,' said Henry. 'I've got an idea about interviewing famous people. They do that in newspapers.'

'I bet she's not come to complain about that ole cat,' said William. 'Jumble's not chased it for days an' days an' she always comes round about it at once.'

'What's she come about, then?' said Ginger.

'I bet she's come to talk about that man that's taken the cottage nex' hers. She's always talkin' about him.'

'I know . . . He's called Mr Helston,' said Henry, 'an' he wont' have anythin' to do with her.'

'No, I wouldn't either if I was him,' said Ginger.

'He won't have anythin' to do with anyone,' said Henry. 'He's a misanthropologist.'

'I bet that word's not right,' said Ginger uncertainly.

'Parts of it are,' said Henry after a moment's consideration.

'Anyway, ole Milly's got all fussed up 'cause he won't get his windows cleaned,' said William. 'I've heard her talkin' about it in the post-office.'

'She's bats,' said Ginger.

'She's givin' a cocktail party tomorrow,' said Henry, 'an' no one wants to go to it but they've got to.'

'I bet that's what she's come for,' said William. 'Borrowin' those silly little glasses, same as they all do when they give cocktail parties. Gosh! You couldn't get a decent drink out of those silly little glasses even if you tried. When I'm grown-up an' have cocktail parties I'll jus' pass the bottles round an' let 'em drink out of them in turns same as we do with lem'nade. There's some *sense* in that.'

'An' proper things to eat with them,' said Douglas. 'Cream buns an' doughnuts an' jellies an' ice-cream things . . . '

William agreed absently. A thoughtful look had come into his face. He had taken a short cut across Miss Milton's garden when 'scouting' Ginger yesterday evening. It was possible that Miss Milton had seen him and come to report the fact to his mother.

'Let's clear off quick to the old barn,' he said. 'Anyway we want to be private. We don't want people int'ruptin' us. I bet the editors of *The Times* an' – an' – an'—'

'The *Poultry World*,' suggested Douglas whose mother kept hens, and studied the *Poultry World* assiduously each week.

'Yes, the *Poultry World*,' said William. 'Well, I bet they don't have their mothers shoutin' up at them every minute not to make so much noise. We've got to be *private*, same as the real ones.'

'All right. Come on,' said the others, ready, as ever, for a change of scene and action.

'I'll jus' tear some pages out of my hist'ry exercise book,' said William. 'I've not taken out any of that yet. My arithmetic one's got so thin that ole Frenchie's gettin' sarky about it . . . An' I'll borrow that purple pencil of Robert's. I bet editors use purple pencils.'

He went to Robert's bedroom, found the indelible pencil, paused for a moment before the looking-glass to pencil a luxuriant moustache from lip to mid-cheek, then rejoined the others.

'I bet most editors have moustaches,' he said a little self-consciously. 'Come on. Let's go to the old barn now.'

With Jumble prancing ahead of them as though leading the expedition, they crept quietly down the stairs and out into the garden.

'Come on quick,' said William, hastening his footsteps to the gate, 'I might have trod on some ole plant or other when I went across her garden yesterday. She'd make a fuss even about that, would ole Milly.'

But Miss Milton was not making a fuss about that. Moreover, so much absorbed was she by her theme that she did not even notice the four boys creeping past the window and throwing apprehensive glances at her as she sat talking to Mrs Brown.

'He's been there for a fortnight now,' she said, 'and the place is still absolutely filthy.'

'But does it really matter, Miss Milton?' said Mrs Brown.

'Of course it matters, Mrs Brown,' said Miss Milton. 'Clematis Cottage closely adjoins my own cottage and I feel – I feel *involved* in it somehow. The place had been standing empty for months before he took it and he never got it cleaned up before he came and he hasn't even had a woman to clean it since he's been here. The windows are coated with dirt. Simply *coated*.'

'But if he doesn't mind—' began Mrs Brown.

'Of course he doesn't mind,' said Miss Milton. 'He goes out every day in that dreadful yellow car and whenever I try to speak to him he just vanishes. He never seems to hear a word I say. He never even seems to see me. I can't understand it.'

'Still, he's only taken the cottage for a few weeks,' said Mrs Brown, 'so you won't have to endure it for long.'

'That's not the point,' said Miss Milton. 'The point is that I'm having a party tomorrow – I'm so glad that you can come, by the way—'

'Oh, yes,' said Mrs Brown, trying to sound more enthusiastic than she felt. 'I'm looking forward to it.'

But Miss Milton, intent on her grievance, had no ear for shades of meaning. She waved the interruption aside.

'It's little short of scandalous,' she said. 'Windows coated with dirt. I have some friends coming to the party who have never visited me before and, really, those windows give the whole place the impression of a slum. I don't know *what* they'll think.'

'Probably nothing at all,' said Mrs Brown, but Miss Milton continued with unabated vehemence:

'I've done what I could. I sent my own window cleaner to clean the outside of the windows one morning while Mr Helston was out, but it made little difference. The inside's so coated with dirt that it looks almost as bad as before.'

'Well, you can't do anything more than that, can you?' said Mrs Brown with a smile.

'Yes, I can, Mrs Brown,' said Miss Milton resolutely, 'and I think I'm going to. I refuse to have the whole tone of my party lowered by such an impression of squalor. I refuse to let my friends think that I inhabit a slum.'

Mrs Brown looked at her visitor with concern. It was clear that Miss Milton was becoming obsessed by the state of her neighbour's windows.

'But what can you do, Miss Milton?' she said.

Miss Milton glanced round and sank her voice to a conspiratorial note. There was a feverish glitter in her usually cold and steely eye.

'I can clean them myself,' she said. 'The wretched man

spends all his time fishing. At least he sets off in that appalling yellow car laden with fishing-rods every morning and doesn't come back till evening. And he never shuts up the cottage. I could easily slip into it and clean the windows and be out of it by the time he gets home.'

'I don't think I should do that,' said Mrs Brown doubtfully. 'I think it would be rather foolish.'

'That's what my cousin Julia says – she's staying with me, you know – but I feel so desperate that I'm prepared to stop at nothing. I tell Julia that she need have nothing to do with it, but she insists that if I go to do it she'll come with me.'

'But Miss Milton—'

'It's no use discussing the matter, Mrs Brown. My mind's made up. I've not slept for nights with worrying about it, and if I don't take some active steps my health will be seriously affected.' She rose and gathered up her shopping basket. 'Well, I won't bother you with my troubles any further. I didn't really mean to pour them out on you like this. I only thought I'd call on my way from shopping to make sure that I could count on you for my party tomorrow.'

'Of course,' said Mrs Brown, 'but do put the windows right out of your mind. I'm sure no one would notice them . . . And now let William carry your basket home for you. I think he's upstairs with his friends.' She went into the hall and listened. Something of peace and tranquillity in the atmosphere of the house told her that William was no longer in it. 'He must have gone out. I'm sorry.'

A flash of the old severity returned to Miss Milton's face.

'That's all right, Mrs Brown. I wouldn't trust William even with a shopping basket.'

The Outlaws had made their way through the village and across the field to the old barn. Ginger had left them for a few minutes to pay a flying visit to his home, which they had to pass on their way. He felt slightly jealous of William's moustache and wanted to find some sub-editorial insignia to compete with it. He considered and discarded as unsuitable an old fancy waistcoat of his father's, a trilby hat of his brother's, an alpenstock, a tea-cosy and a – 1940 model – tin hat, appearing finally in a pair of sunglasses of elaborate design that belonged to his mother.

'They've got to have strong glasses, sub-editors,' he explained as he joined the others, ''cause of all this fine work they've got to do – drawin' advertisements an' suchlike.'

William snorted but forbore to make any comment and soon the Outlaws were seated on the ground of the old barn deep in discussion.

'We've got to fix what to call it first,' said William.

'The *Poultry World*,' said Douglas who had been gratified by William's acceptance of his previous suggestion.

'No, you chump!' said William. 'It's not about hens.'

'The *Old Barn Times*,' suggested Henry.

'Yes, that's a jolly good idea,' said William. 'An' now I'm goin' to do the Animals' Corner an' then we'll do the po'm.'

To the accompaniment of pants and groans and a few more All against All wrestling matches the Animals' Corner and the poem were finally completed, and William, over whose face the marks of indelible pencil had spread like a flood, obliterating even his moustache, stood up to read the results to the editorial staff.

'I'll read my Animals' Corner first,' he said, ''cause it's the most important.'

'It jolly well isn't,' said the sub-editor, adjusting his glasses, which had a tendency to slip down over his small snub nose and form a sort of gag over his mouth.

'Yes, it is, an' kin'ly shut up,' said William sternly. 'Kin'ly shut up, all of you, an' listen . . . I've wrote about dogs.' He took the grubby sheet of paper on which he had written his contribution and read aloud in a throaty resonant voice.

'It seems silly to me the fuss some people make about dogs that are only one sort of dogs. Stands to reason that dogs that are all sorts of dogs are more int'restin' than dogs that are only one sort of dogs. We'd all like to have all sorts of dogs but we can't because our parents wouldn't let us an' there wouldn't be room for them but if you can get a dog that's all sorts of dogs in one dog it comes to nearly the same thing as having all sorts of dogs in sep'rate dogs an' so the sort of dog they call a mongrel that's all sorts of dogs in one dog is a jolly sight better than a dog that's only one sort of dog in one dog that they make such a fuss about. That's as far as I got.'

Jumble assumed a coy expression and wagged his tail approvingly. The others clapped.

'Yes, I think it's jolly good, too,' said William modestly, bowing his recognition of the applause. 'An' now I'll read the po'm. It got into a bit of a muddle when we wrote it but I bet I can get it straight readin' it. It's a jolly good po'm. I like that bit I did best.' He quelled the rising murmur of dissent by a stern 'Shut up an' listen', and, adopting the high-pitched voice that he considered suitable for poetry, read:

'Flowers come springin' out in the spring,
An' Shakespeare wrote about love an' said it was a
   jolly good thing,
An' I'm goin' to be the first one to shoot myself to
   the moon,
An' choc'late creams taste better than lollipops
   though they get finished more soon.'

Loud cheers greeted the recital and, following William's example, the Outlaws stood up and bowed to each other with varying degrees of ungainliness.

'Mine's the only bit that sounded like real po'try,' said Henry complacently as they sat down again.

'Gosh, *mine* did,' said Ginger. 'If real po'try isn't about love, I don't know what is.'

'I like my bit,' said Douglas reflectively.

'They were all jolly good,' said William, who, as editor, felt that enough time had been wasted in argument and wrestling matches and that they should get down to the matter in hand. 'I think it's goin' to be the best newspaper we've ever done.'

'It's better than the las' one,' agreed Ginger.

'Violet Elizabeth messed that one up,' said William. 'Thank goodness she's not here to mess up this one!'

'Hello, William,' said a voice of plaintive sweetness behind them. They turned with gasps of horror to see Violet Elizabeth standing in the doorway.

'Go away!' said William sternly. 'We don't want you.'

'I don't mind, William,' said Violet Elizabeth serenely, advancing into the barn and taking her place among the editorial staff between William and Ginger.

'Go away!' said William.

'Yeth, William,' said Violet Elizabeth meekly.

'Well, *go*!' said William.

'Yeth, William,' said Violet Elizabeth, crossing her feet, tailor-fashion, and obviously settling down for a prolonged visit.

'Push her out,' said Ginger.

'If you try to puth me out,' said Violet Elizabeth sweetly, 'I'll—'

'Oh, all right,' capitulated William. Violet Elizabeth's screams were of such strength and volume that they had been known to bring would-be rescuers to her aid from every corner of the village. 'Come on. Let's take no notice of her. Let's jus' go on as if she wasn't here.'

The others agreed a little doubtfully. It was a manoeuvre they had tried on many similar occasions and generally without success.

'If people haven't got enough *p'liteness* to go away when other people tell them they don't want them,' said William, 'then – then – well, they haven't got any p'liteness,' he ended somewhat lamely.

'Yeth, William,' said Violet Elizabeth. 'I don't mind, William. What are you doing, William?'

'Shan't tell you,' said William, removing himself and his staff to the further end of the barn. 'Now come on. We're goin' to go on jus' as if she wasn't here. What shall we have next? After the Animal Corner an' the po'm.'

'They have interviews with famous people in real newspapers same as I said,' said Henry. 'I once saw one of 'em doin' it in the pictures. They take out their paper an' pencil an' they say: I represent the – the *Old Barn Times*, we'd say – an' then ask them a question. That's what they do in real newspapers.'

'Now I know what you're doing,' said Violet Elizabeth with quiet triumph. 'You're doing a newthpaper.'

'You shut up,' said William, then, turning to the others, 'Yes, that's a good idea. Let's think what to ask them.'

'You ought to have crimthe in a newthpaper, William,' said Violet Elizabeth.

'*Gosh!*' said William, as a faint and distant memory became clearer. 'That's what you said the las' time we had one! An' you did one, too.'

'It wath only a little one, William,' said Violet Elizabeth apologetically. 'I'll do a bigger one for thith newthpaper, William.'

'You jolly well *won't*!' said William.

'I puthed a man off a thile and took his purthe,' said Violet Elizabeth reminiscently. 'It wath a very little purthe. I'm older now, William. I can do a bigger one.'

'Will – you – go – away!' said William savagely.

'All right, William,' said Violet Elizabeth, rising to her feet and trotting out of the barn door.

They watched her retreating figure with mingled relief and incredulity.

'Good riddance!' said William.

'Yes, if it *is* riddance,' said Henry, voicing their secret doubts.

'Well, she's gone, anyway,' said William, 'so let's get on with this interview thing . . . It's goin' to be jolly difficult to find a famous person to start with. Famous people are all in London – in the House of Lords and in Television and places like that.'

'Well, we *might* meet one,' said Henry, 'an' we ought to have the question ready for when we do.'

'All right. Let's think of one.'

They thought in silence for a moment or two – a silence broken only by the snorts and hard breathing that always accompanied their mental efforts.

'What sort of sweets do you like best,' suggested Douglas whose mind was still running on the line that he had contributed to the composite poem.

'No, you chump!' said William. 'That's a batty question. Let's have another think.'

They had another think in the course of which William sucked his pencil so hard that a fresh tide of purple spread over his face.

'I've thought of one,' said Henry. 'Let's ask him if he doesn't think that homework ought to be done away with by lor.'

'No, that wouldn't do,' said William. 'It's a jolly important question but famous people wouldn't be int'rested in it. They've all left school so it doesn't matter to them now. Let's think again.'

This time it was Ginger who broke the silence.

'Let's ask him that riddle about what's the difference between an apple and an elephant.'

'*No!*' said William. 'Tell you what ! I've got an idea. Let's ask him what's the most exciting moment of his life.'

'Yes, that's a jolly good one,' admitted Ginger.

'I think ith a nithe one, too, William,' said a well-known voice behind them.

Groaning, they turned to see Violet Elizabeth once more standing in the doorway. She carried a brown attaché case and smiled on them benignly.

'Gosh! I thought you'd *gone*,' said William in a tone of deep disgust.

'I only went to do a crime for the newthpaper,' said Violet Elizabeth, walking into the barn and putting the attaché case down at William's feet. 'You've *got* to have crimthe for newthpaperth, William, or elth people wouldn't read them. I've done a nithe big one thith time. I only did thuth a little one latht time.'

William threw a harassed look at the case.

'Gosh, Violet Elizabeth, d'you mean—'

Violet Elizabeth beamed at him proudly.

'Yeth, William. I thtole it. I thtole it out of a motor-car. You *can't* have a newthpaper without thomeone thtealing thomething out of a motor-car. Therth alwayth thomething about thomeone thtealing thomething out of a motor-car in a newthpaper. I heard my mummy thay tho. Tho I thtole it.'

William's face was blank with horror.

'Well, we've jus' got to take it back as quick as we can,' he said. 'Serve you right if you had to go to prison, Violet Elizabeth.'

'I thouldn't mind going to prithon, William,' said Violet Elizabeth serenely. 'I thouldn't have to drink malt ecthract in prithon. I don't like malt ecthract.'

VIOLET ELIZABETH PUT THE ATTACHÉ CASE DOWN AT
WILLIAM'S FEET. 'I THTOLE IT,' SHE SAID PROUDLY.

'What sort of car was it an' where was it?' demanded
William sternly.

'It wath a yellow car, William, with fithing-rodth in it and it
wath outthide the potht-offith. It wath a very thabby car.'

'It mus' have been Mr Helston's,' said William. 'The man
that's living in that cottage nex' Miss Milton's.'

'Clematis Cottage.'

'Yes . . . Come on. Let's take it back quick.'

'Thath very thilly after all the trouble I've taken thtealing it,' said Violet Elizabeth reproachfully, but they brushed her aside and, snatching up the case, ran across the field to the village street. The street was empty; there was no sign of the yellow car in front of the post-office.

'Gosh!' they panted in dismay.

There was a baffled air even about Jumble as he sat down to scratch his ear in the middle of the road.

'He's gone,' said William. 'What are we goin' to do now?'

'Let's take it to Clematis Cottage,' said Henry.

But a visit to Clematis Cottage was fruitless. No one answered their knock. Mr Helston had evidently gone off for his day's fishing.

'We'll take it back to the old barn an' keep it for him till he comes home,' said William.

They returned to the old barn, where they found Violet Elizabeth hopping about on one leg in a carefree fashion.

'I'm having a hopping rathe againtht mythelf, William,' she said. 'I've jutht done theven and a half hopth without putting my foot down.'

'You ought to be in the Tower of London,' said William severely. 'That's where you ought to be.'

'Yeth, William,' said Violet Elizabeth and began another hopping race, considerably hampered by Jumble's efforts to join in.

'Now let's get on with this newspaper,' said William, setting down the case and taking up the scattered pieces of grubby paper on which their journalistic efforts were inscribed. 'Let's think of what to have next.'

But their interests in the newspaper had waned. Their eyes kept wandering to the brown attaché case.

'Wonder what's in it,' said Henry.

'Might be his tea,' said Ginger.

'Well, if it is, I don't s'pose he'd mind us eatin' it,' said

Douglas. 'It'd prob'ly be bad by the time he gets back. It'd save it goin' bad if we et it.'

'Might be part of his fishin' stuff,' said Henry. 'Bait an' stuff . . . '

'It'd be int'restin' to have a look at 'em,' said Ginger in a detached sort of voice.

'I bet it's locked,' said Douglas.

'There wouldn't be any harm in seein' whether it's locked or not. If it's somethin' valu'ble we ought to take more care of it than if it isn't.'

'Yes, come on,' said the others, their scruples vanishing.

William took the attaché case and slid the catches. It was not locked. Four heads bent over it eagerly as William opened the lid . . . then the tension relaxed. There came four groans of disappointment.

'Only papers! An' not many of them!'

'Well, let's see what's in 'em,' said Ginger. 'I think we ought to 'cause of what you said about takin' more care of them if they're valu'ble than if they aren't.'

'A'right,' agreed William, obviously ready to yield to persuasion.

He took out the handful of papers and began to read them. As he read, his eyes widened and his mouth dropped open.

'Gosh, it's his diary,' he said, 'an' – *Gosh!* He's a *murderer!*'

They craned their necks over his shoulder again, reading the manuscript.

'My sister Mirabel and I have now been in Clematis Cottage for about a fortnight. We left our last home in somewhat of a hurry, but so far no one has connected us with the mysterious death of our aunt whose money we now find so useful. Mirabel was very clever over that affair. She used a rare poison that had been brought over from Africa . . . '

'He's a *murderer*,' said William again hoarsely. He turned

over the pages. 'The rest's jus' tellin' about the village an' the country an' that sort of thing. He's got all about the pond an' the stepping stones over the river an' the railway bridge an' ole Jenks' scarecrows . . . Gosh! Fancy him bein' a murderer an' goin' fishin' an' things jus' as if he wasn't!'

'We once thought Archie was a crim'nal an' he turned out not to be,' Henry reminded him.

'Yes, but this is *diff'rent*,' said William. 'He's wrote it down in axshul *words*. We can't have made a mistake this time.'

'But he says he's got his sister Mirabel with him in the cottage,' objected Ginger, 'an' he hasn't got any sister with him there. He's stayin' there alone.'

'How d'you know he is?' challenged William. 'Have you been all over the cottage an' looked under the beds an' everywhere? Well, it's news to *me* if you've been all over the cottage an' looked under the beds and everywhere . . . '*Course* he's got his sister hid there. I bet you anythin' she's hidin' there under a bed or somethin' so's the p'lice won't find her. He doesn't have anyone to clean out the cottage an' he keeps his windows dirty, same as Miss Milton said, so's no one can look in an' see this Mirabel, 'cause if the p'lice are after him, they'll be lookin' for a murderer with a sister, not a murderer all by himself . . . Anyway, they're both murderers. He said so. An' his sister's a worse murderer than what he is, 'cause she got this poison from Africa.'

'Well, what are we goin' to do?' said Ginger. 'Shall we write to Scotland Yard?'

'No,' said William after a moment's consideration. 'We'll go an' find out about it ourselves. It'll be a jolly good thing for our newspaper. It'll be a snook, same as Henry said.'

'Scoop,' said Henry.

'Well, whatever it is it'll be it. We'll be the first to find out about it an' we'll have it in our newspaper before any of the other newspapers an' it'll make us famous all over the world.'

'I bet this sister's gone by now even if she was there,' said Henry. 'It'd be jus' our luck to find she'd gone.'

'Let's go 'n' see,' said William. 'He's gone out fishin' an' I bet he'll stay out all day. He always does. Let's go 'n' see if the sister's in the cottage.'

'It might be a bit dangerous,' said Douglas.

' 'Course it'll be dangerous,' said William. 'We'll be goin' right into the jaws of death. Murderers like that stick at nothin'. They're jus' as likely to jab this African poison into us as into that ole aunt they murdered. But I bet real newspaper people don't mind a bit of danger. I bet the editor of *The Times* an' – an' the *Poultry World* wouldn't stop goin' into a cottage after a murderer for a scoop jus' 'cause they might get a bit of poison jabbed into 'em . . . Anyway, I'm goin' there, an' the rest of you needn't come if you don't want to.'

''Course we'll come,' said the others, and Jumble leaped up and down in happy anticipation.

'We'll take Jumble,' said William. 'There's a good bit of bloodhound in him an' he'll be jolly useful. He only hasn't caught a crim'nal yet 'cause he's never had a chance to get near enough to one. I bet he'll catch this African murderer all right.' He took up the case. 'Well, come on.'

'Can I come, too, pleathe, William?' said Violet Elizabeth. 'I won't be a nuithanthe.'

'No,' said William sternly. 'We don't want you an' you can jus' keep out of it.'

'Yeth, William,' said Violet Elizabeth meekly, taking up her position at the rear of the procession and obviously preparing to follow it across the field.

'Come on,' said William again. 'We'll jus' take no notice of her.'

* * *

Clematis Cottage was apparently deserted. The Outlaws approached it cautiously from the back, William leading the way, followed in single file by Ginger, Henry, Douglas and Violet Elizabeth. Jumble brought up the rear. His excitement had died down, but his face wore an eager expression as if he were ready to enjoy whatever adventures Fate had in store for him.

'I'm goin' to try the back door,' said William, 'an' if it's locked we'll climb up by the bathroom window.'

'I bet there's no one in,' said Henry.

'I think we ought to've come armed,' said Douglas a little nervously. 'That water-pistol of mine'd pretty well brain anyone if I shot it hard enough. I'd have brought it along with me if I'd known.'

'I'll put my tongue out at them ath far ath it will go, thall I, William?' said Violet Elizabeth.

'Shut up!' hissed William.

He tried the door. It opened. The procession crept into the untidy disordered kitchen. Violet Elizabeth looked about her in frowning disapproval.

'What a meth!' she said disdainfully.

'Shut up!' said William again in a piercing whisper.

He went to the door that led into the little hall and stood there listening.

Through the empty house came the distant murmur of a woman's voice.

'Mirabel!' gasped the little crowd.

Douglas had turned pale.

'If she squirts that African poison through a syringe, I don't see how she can miss us,' he said. 'I think we'd better go an' tell the p'lice.'

'Shut up an' listen,' said William.

Again the murmur of a woman's voice reached them from a room overhead.

'There mus' be more than one of them,' said Henry. 'She couldn't be talkin' to herself.'

'Thee can't have wathed-up for *dayth*,' said Violet Elizabeth, throwing a glance of pained fastidiousness at the sink.

Jumble, whose head had disappeared into the rubbish pail, emerged with the remains of a mutton chop and lay down under the kitchen table to deal with it.

'Yes, there's two voices,' whispered Henry.

'There's prob'ly a gang of them,' said William. 'Let's go 'n' see what they're doin' . . . Come on, quietly . . . Don't make a sound.'

Pulling up his coat collar as if to conceal his identity, his face set and scowling, the tip of his tongue protruding as it generally did in moments of tension, walking on tiptoe in an ungainly high-stepping fashion, he led his band down the hall and up the stairs. They followed, unconsciously adopting his expression and gait – all except Violet Elizabeth, who kept passing her finger over banisters and picture frames, regarding its resultant grubby state with little tut-tuts of disapproval. Jumble once more brought up the rear, carrying his chop bone in his mouth.

William stopped outside a closed door at the top of the stairs and applied his ear to it.

'They're in here,' he whispered.

'The key's in the lock,' whispered Henry.

William looked at the key . . . and on a sudden impulse turned it.

'Got 'em,' he said.

'Well, don't leave the key in the lock,' said Douglas. 'Burglars push it out an' get it back if you do.'

'All right.'

William took out the key, looked vaguely round, then put it on a small chest of drawers on the landing near him.

'What'll we do now?' whispered Ginger.

'Come on in here,' said William, leading the way to a small bedroom across the landing.

It was evidently the bedroom occupied by Mr Helston. A dressing-gown was flung across the bed. Boots and shoes and various articles of clothing lay about in disorder. William shepherded his flock inside and closed the door.

'Well, we've captured and imprisoned 'em all right,' he said.

'Yes, but what are we goin' to do next?' said Ginger, adjusting his sunglasses. 'They don't seem to know they're captured and imprisoned. What are we goin' to *do*?'

'Well, wait a *minute*,' said William a little irritably. 'I can't think of everythin' at once.' The task of discovering whether or not Mirabel was concealed in Clematis Cottage had bounded his mental horizon. Now that Mirabel – and her presumed confederate – had been not only discovered but imprisoned, he found himself for the moment at a loss. 'Anyway, we've got 'em locked up an' they can't get out, so there's heaps of time to fix up what to do with 'em.'

Violet Elizabeth was examining the fireplace, which was full of fallen soot, torn-up envelopes, used matches, and empty cigarette cartons.

'What a meth!' she said. 'And look at all thith thoot! I don't think they've had the chimney thwept for yearth.'

She put her head into the chimney-hole to investigate and received a fresh fall of soot full in her face. The Outlaws' titters were firmly checked by William.

'I don't mind,' she said placidly, surveying her blackened features in the mirror. 'It lookth nither than William'th 'cauthe William'th ith only penthil and minthe thoot.'

'What's the good of capturin' people if they don't know they're captured?' said Ginger again.

'Listen. I've got an idea,' said William. 'We've got to let

WILLIAM SLIPPED THE SHEETS OF PAPER UNDER THE DOOR.

them know that the game's up an' we're on their tracks.'

'Let's go in an' tell 'em, then,' said Henry.

'No, we don't want them to know that we're not grown-ups,' said William. 'If they thought we weren't grown-ups they mightn't take any notice of us. But this idea of mine's a jolly good one. Now listen.' He opened the attaché case and took out the sheets of paper. 'I'm goin' to slip this under the door, then they'll know that someone knows all about them an' is on their tracks an' I bet they'll be so scared they'll jus' confess everythin' an' s'render. It's worth tryin' anyway.'

They watched him anxiously as he tiptoed across the landing and slipped the sheets of paper under the door.

'They'll know the game's up now,' he said as he rejoined

the others. 'They'll prob'ly think they're surrounded by Scotland Yard . . . We'll wait an' see what happens.'

Miss Milton and her cousin had entered Clematis Cottage carrying a bowl of water and a couple of wash leathers.

'We'll start upstairs, Julia,' said Miss Milton. 'It's the upstairs windows that are most noticeable from the road and that give such a bad impression.'

'You know, Mildred, I still don't think that we ought to,' said the cousin. 'Suppose Mr Helston comes back . . .'

'Of course he won't, Julia,' said Miss Milton, who had screwed up her courage to such an extent that nothing now would have prevented her from carrying out the enterprise. 'He's gone out fishing and he never gets back till dusk.'

She entered the small front bedroom whose window was most conspicuous from the road and looked about her.

'He evidently lives in this room. Books and letters and pipes and things. And remains of a meal. What a pigsty! . . . Now let's start on the windows. Here's a wash leather for you, Julia.' She attacked the window with concentrated energy. 'You know, the dirt's simply *ingrained*. We shall be lucky if we get even one coating of it off.'

She continued to work, assisted in a half-hearted fashion by her cousin.

'Ingrained!' she repeated at intervals. 'Simply ingrained!'

Then she noticed that Julia was standing motionless in a listening attitude.

'What's the matter, dear?'

'I thought I heard someone in the house,' said Julia. 'In fact I'm sure I did . . . You're a little deaf, dear, so you probably heard nothing, but I've been hearing movements and whispering for some time.'

Miss Milton gave a gasp of horror.

'Mr Helston!' she said.

'No, it can't be Mr Helston . . . He wouldn't move about in such a furtive fashion. I can't hear anything just at the moment, but I'm sure I heard what sounded like several people creeping upstairs and whispering.'

'Merciful Heavens!' said Miss Milton. 'Burglars!'

'Yes, I don't see what else it could be,' said Julia. 'What shall we do?'

'Nothing, Julia,' said Miss Milton, lowering her voice to a whisper. 'It isn't our house and anyway there's nothing worth stealing in it. The important thing is to conceal our presence here at all costs. You know what these modern burglars are, Julia. They all carry coshes and lead piping and razors and pistols as a matter of course. Our lives wouldn't be worth an instant's purchase if they found us here. I'm going to hide behind this curtain and you must hide behind that one – we'll get covered with dust but that can't be helped . . . and we won't move or speak till the thieves have gone.'

'I'm just going to peep out and see what's happening,' said Julia.

'Julia, don't! I implore you!'

But Julia was already at the door, turning the handle.

'It won't open,' she said. 'It's locked . . . Mildred, we're locked in.'

Miss Milton came out of her hiding-place. There was a wild and dishevelled look about her usually trim figure.

'We're trapped,' she said, trying the handle in her turn. 'They've locked us in, Julia, so that they can ransack the place in safety and deal with us later. No one will ever know what happened to us . . . I haven't even got a hatpin to defend myself with.' She gave a stifled scream. 'Look, Julia! Look! They've pushed some papers under the door.'

Miss Milton's courage was ebbing. Her voice quavered on a shrill tremolo.

She picked up the pages of typescript.

'I can't read it,' she whispered. 'I haven't got my glasses. Can you read it, Julia?'

'No,' said Julia. 'I haven't got mine, either.'

'I'm going to put it in my handbag,' whispered Miss Milton through chattering teeth. 'It may prove to be a clue in bringing the criminal to justice . . . that is, if we survive to assist in bringing them to justice – if we are ever seen or heard of again after this ghastly experience. Come back quickly into hiding, Julia. It's our only hope of safety and a slender one at that.'

'Well, they've not s'rendered yet,' said Ginger.

'They've prob'ly got some of that African poison still hid about somewhere,' said Douglas nervously. He dived into a corner of the room and emerged with a long narrow wastepaper-basket. 'I'm goin' to put this on.' He drew it with some difficulty over his head. 'It'll be a sort of protection if they start syringing that poison about.'

'That won't keep it off,' said Henry, 'an' it's the *fumes* of poison that's the deadliest an' you can only keep fumes off by wearing gauze stuff over your mouth an' nose, same as doctors an' firemen.' His eyes rested on the bedraggled lace 'runner' of the dressing-table, and, after a moment's hesitation, he took it up and tied it round his nose and mouth. 'Like this,' he ended in a muffled voice.

'Now listen,' said William. 'We can't keep on an' on wasting time. I vote we go to them an' tell them they're imprisoned and surrounded an' ask them to s'render.'

'An' what if they won't?' said Ginger.

'We'll attack in force an' overpower them. Jumble can do his bloodhound stuff. I bet that'll scare them.'

'I bet Jumble won't . . . Where is he, anyway?'

Jumble, who had gone under the bed to demolish what was left of his chop bone, came out, waving his tail.

'Yes, he *looks* a bloodhound, doesn't he?' said Ginger sarcastically.

'You wait! You watch!' said William, rising passionately to the defence of his pet. 'I'll jus' give him a bit of practice first.' He took a cushion from a chair and held it up by the corner. 'Go on, boy! At it boy! Cats, Jumble! Rats, Jumble!'

Without a moment's hesitation Jumble flung himself upon the cushion – less because of any strong bloodhound strain in his constitution than because he always enjoyed investigating the interiors of cushions – ripping open the cover and plunging joyously into clouds of kapok stuffing.

'There!' said William triumphantly. 'I said he'd scare 'em.'

'Pleathe, can I be a bloodhound, too, William?' put in Violet Elizabeth.

'*No!*'

'Well, he hasn't scared anyone yet,' said Ginger. 'He's only torn up a cushion an' I bet we'll get in a row for it.'

'I bet we'll get in a row anyway,' said Douglas indistinctly. He wrestled in silence with his wastepaper-basket for a few moments.

There came the sound of a car at the gate and Henry went to the window.

'I say, William,' he said. 'Here's Mr Helston back in his car, an' – *Gosh*, William, your father's with him.'

Mr Helston's car, winding its leisurely way from the river, had developed a puncture, and Mr Brown, on his way home from the station, had given a hand with changing the tyre.

'It's very good of you,' said Mr Helston when the operation was completed. 'Actually the spare's got a slow puncture, too. I meant to get it mended and kept forgetting.'

'Why not run it along to the garage now?' said Mr Brown. 'They won't take long mending it.'

'Right!' agreed Mr Helston. He was a tall lanky man with

greying hair and a thin pleasant face. 'And may I give you a lift if it's on your way?'

It was on Mr Brown's way, so the two of them drove back together to the village.

They got on extremely well. It turned out that Mr Helston – under another name – was the author of a series of books on the English Counties that Mr Brown had read with great enjoyment.

'Are you taking a holiday here?' said Mr Brown when he had complimented the author and discussed the various numbers of the series.

'Yes,' said Mr Helston. 'I'd been working rather too hard on my last book to get it ready in time for publication this year, and my doctor ordered me a complete rest, so I thought I'd come to some out-of-the-way place where no one knew me and devote my time to fishing. I think you're about the first person I've spoken to since I came here. I haven't even got a daily woman – I believe the place is filthy if one bothered to notice it – and I've been revelling in an atmosphere of unalloyed peace.'

'You don't find that it palls?' said Mr Brown.

'I didn't at first,' said Mr Helston. 'Complete idleness seemed to satisfy every need of my nature, but last night I did begin to feel that I'd like to get my teeth into something, so I started a thriller.'

'A thriller?'

'Yes. I've always thought I'd like to try my hand at one. I only wrote half a chapter and even that tailed off into a description of the countryside. I thought I'd use this village as a background to the story, and, once I'd got going on the scenery, I seemed to forget all about the story. I suppose the leopard can't change its spots. It was a rotten story anyway.'

'I'm sure it wasn't.' said Mr Brown. 'I hope you'll go on with it.'

'I can't,' said Mr Helston. 'It's been stolen. I thought I'd take it down to the river with me and get on with it in the intervals of fishing, but I called at the post-office on my way and when I came out the case had been stolen from my car.' He smiled. 'The thief will feel a little sold when he finds that his only "bag" is a few pages of worthless manuscript.'

'And serve him right!' said Mr Brown sternly.

Mr Helston had drawn up at the gate of Clematis Cottage.

'Come in and have a drink before we go on to the garage,' he said. 'I find that I'm beginning to hanker after human companionship again. My cure must be complete.'

'Splendid!' said Mr Brown.

'The place is all at sixes and sevens, of course,' said Mr Helston. 'I haven't dusted or washed-up properly since I've been in it. I live in one of the upstairs rooms. I always like an upstairs sitting-room or study. One feels more cut off from the world.'

Mr Brown had got out of the car and was looking at it in a contemplative fashion.

'It was pinking pretty badly as we came along, wasn't it?'

'Yes, it does,' said Mr Helston simply.

'I'd like just to have a look at the plugs, if I may. It won't take me a minute.'

'Right. Very good of you. I'll go upstairs and rake out the bottle and glasses and do a spot of tidying so as not to give you too much of a shock . . . Come straight upstairs when you're ready.'

Mr Helston ran upstairs three steps at a time and turned the handle of the door. A puzzled expression came over his face. It was locked. He knew he hadn't locked it. He never locked doors. As he stood there puzzling over the situation, his ear caught the sound of furtive movement and lowered voices from inside the room. His puzzled expression changed to one of indignation. He rattled the door sharply.

'Open this door at once, whoever's inside there!' he called.

He was answered by a low moan – the opening note of Miss Milton's hysterics.

It was at this point that he noticed the key on the chest of drawers. He turned it in the lock and flung open the door. The shock was so great that Miss Milton stopped midway in her attack of hysterics. At first he saw no one in the room . . . then he noticed the two substantial bulges behind the curtains, each ending in a pair of stout brown walking shoes.

He strode across the room and drew back the curtains, then stood staring in blank surprise at the two prim middle-aged ladies exposed to view.

'May I ask what you are doing here?' he said.

He did not recognise Miss Milton as his next door neighbour. He knew that he had a next door neighbour but he had never noticed her features.

'What is the meaning of this?' he continued, his indignation mounting at this flagrant intrusion on his privacy.

Miss Milton opened her mouth to speak but only strange incomprehensible sounds issued from it. Julia took charge of the situation.

'Please listen,' she said in a trembling voice. 'My cousin lives next door to you. We can prove our identity. Where is your handbag, Mildred? . . . Look! Here is an envelope with her name and address . . . '

She opened the handbag and rummaged for the letter, but Mr Helston had seized the sheets of typescript that fell from the bag. He examined them, an expression of amazed severity on his face.

'And how does it come,' he said slowly, 'that the papers stolen from my car this morning are in your bag? I should like to hear what explanation you have to offer before I put the matter in the hands of the police.'

'Police?' screamed Julia. 'I don't understand. I—'

'I REPRESENT THE "OLD BARN TIMES",' SAID WILLIAM.

Miss Milton had abandoned herself to her hysterics. They gathered force . . . then stopped abruptly as a well-known voice came from half way down the stairs.

'The plugs are filthy,' called Mr Brown cheerfully, 'and I think she's only running on two cylinders.'

He entered the room and stood looking round in surprise.

'These are the thieves who stole the attaché case from my car,' said Mr Helston. 'They appear to have had the further bright idea of breaking into my cottage.'

'Good Lord!' said Mr Brown. 'Miss Milton!'

Miss Milton, who had still not recovered the power of

speech, uttered sounds suggestive of the bleating of a mountain goat.

Suddenly the door of the opposite room burst open and the Outlaws, Violet Elizabeth and Jumble poured out.

'Be careful, Dad,' panted William. 'He's a murderer. They're both murderers – him and his sister. They've murdered their aunt an' they've got some African poison with them.' He looked round the room. 'Where's Mirabel? Where is she? We heard her in here a moment ago.'

'Mirabel?' said Mr Helston with dawning comprehension and amusement in his voice.

'Yes,' said William. 'We've read your diary an' we know all about you an' your sister Mirabel murderin' your aunt an'—'

'I don't know how you got here, William,' said Mr Brown looking down at the empurpled features of his son, 'or how you come to be in this appalling state, or whether you are in any way responsible for this extraordinary situation, but let me inform you that Mr Helston is a well-known writer, whose books thousands of people besides myself have read with profit and pleasure.'

William gazed at him open-mouthed.

'D'you mean he's famous?'

'Of course he's famous,' said Mr Brown.

Without a moment's hesitation, William dragged from his pocket the grubby piece of paper and much-bitten pencil that formed his editorial equipment.

'I represent the *Old Barn Times*,' he said. 'Can you kin'ly tell me—' The other four joined in, Violet Elizabeth's voice rising shrilly above the chorus, 'what is the mos' excitin' moment of your life?'

Mr Helston's gaze went to William, his features barely discernible beneath their purple covering . . . to Ginger, whose sunglasses had again slipped down over his mouth . . . to

Douglas still encased in his wastepaper-basket . . . to Henry, the lace runner dangling from one ear . . . to Violet Elizabeth, smiling sweetly through a mask of soot . . . to Jumble, shaking tufts of kapok from his fur and chasing them round the room . . . to Miss Milton, who was taking up her hysterics at the point where she had left them off . . . to Mr Brown, who was looking at them all in a stupefied fashion.

'On the whole, I think, this one,' he said.

Chapter 6

William and the Old Boy

William walked slowly along the road, his hands in his pockets, his toes dragging through the dust, his eyes fixed on the ground in a thoughtful frown.

He was on his way home from a particularly painful interview with the headmaster – the result of a series of unsatisfactory reports from Mr French, William's form master – and was solacing himself with various daydreams suitable to the occasion. The most satisfactory was one in which the headmaster came to him in a state of abject terror, explaining that he had committed a crime, that the police were on his tracks and begging William to give him shelter and find him a hiding-place. He implored forgiveness for all his unkindness and pleaded for help.

'You're the only boy in the school I can count on,' he said. 'As soon as I heard that Scotland Yard was after me, I said to myself, "Brown's the boy to go to. Brown will know what to do. Brown will get me out of this scrape. Brown will forgive me all the wrong I've done him and save me from my dreadful fate . . . " You will help me, won't you, Brown? I daren't trust myself to any other. You're the one boy in the school I can turn to.'

The abject, grovelling Mr Marks was a pleasant picture to contemplate, and William contemplated it with pleasure, raising his drooping figure and beginning to swagger down the road.

Then he proceeded to rally and encourage the criminal.

'Yes, I'll forgive you,' he said magnanimously, 'but' – repeating, as far as he remembered them, the words the headmaster had used in the recent interview – 'I hope this'll be a lesson to you and that you'll conduct yourself different in future . . . An' come on. I know a place where I can hide you an' where no one'll find you an' I'll bring you food an' you can hide up there till it's all blown over.'

Mr Marks stammered broken words of gratitude and William led the cringing figure across the field in the shelter of the hedge to the old barn.

'You'll be all right here,' he said. 'If Scotland Yard comes after you jus' hide under those sacks in the corner. I've hid there lots of times an' no one's found me. Now I'll go home for tea an' I'll come back with a bun or somethin' for you.'

Nearing the gate of his house, William informed an imaginary policeman that he had seen a man who might have been Mr Marks going down the road in the direction of the aerodrome and that he was probably by now in a Comet on his way to France. He watched the policeman set off at a run in the direction of the aerodrome, and, smiling triumphantly, entered his home.

A large plate of raspberry buns – freshly made by Mrs Brown – drove everything else from his mind for the first five minutes; then, the edge of his appetite blunted, his thoughts turned again to the picture of Mr Marks, cowering in a corner of the old barn . . . He had promised him a bun. He slipped a bun into his pocket. The real and imaginary often became so closely merged in William's mind that he found it a little difficult to disentangle them. He finished the last crumb of the last bun on the plate, resisted the temptation to eat Mr Marks's bun, and made his way across the field to the old barn.

He entered it with a careless swagger, then stopped on the

threshold, open-mouthed with amazement. For Mr Marks was in the barn, not cowering in the corner but standing in the middle, looking around him.

'Ah, Brown,' he said vaguely. 'Perhaps you can help me.' He took a letter from his pocket. 'I've heard from James Aloysius Worfield – an old boy of apparently unlimited wealth – who is proposing to visit the school. He was before my time, so I don't know him, but' – he turned over a page of the letter – 'he hints that he would like to present the school with some tangible memorial of his visit. A pavilion for the playing fields is the idea that occurs to me, but I realise that the gentleman must be handled carefully. He says that he hopes to find the landmarks of his boyhood unchanged. He gives a list of them and I thought I'd check up on them personally before answering the letter.' He scanned the pages again. 'He mentions first the old barn . . . This is the old barn, I presume?'

'Yes, but it's our place,' said William a little indignantly. 'We always play here.'

'Doubtless, my boy. Doubtless. But when you in your turn are a prosperous city gentleman or an ornament to some learned profession—'

'I'm going to be a diver, sir.'

'Yes, yes . . . well, the particular sphere on which you shed lustre by your presence does not affect the situation. Other boys will still play here and regard it as their property.'

'Yes, I suppose so, sir,' said William, surprised and a little outraged by the idea.

'The old barn, then, I may tick off . . . Perhaps you can help me with the others.' He consulted the letter again. 'The tree with the hole in its trunk in Crown Woods . . . '

'Yes, sir. That's still there.'

'The ruined cottage with the apple trees down in the valley . . . '

'Yes, sir.'

'The stepping stones over the river . . . '

'Yes, sir.'

Mr Marks folded up his letter.

'That's all right, then. I can tell the gentleman that his landmarks still stand . . . I'm not looking forward to his visit. He sounds a typical example of the class of moneyed Old Boy – class I find particularly tiresome. However, one should not say such things, so we'll consider it unsaid. Now don't let me keep you from your business, whatever it is. By the way, what did you come for?'

'I came to bring you a bun,' said William.

'That was kind of you,' said Mr Marks mildly. 'How did you know I'd be here?'

'I hid you here,' said William. 'I mean, you'd got into trouble with the p'lice an' you came – I mean, I sort of pretended you came – an' said you were sorry about this afternoon an' asked me to hide you an' put the p'lice off an' I hid you here an' told the p'lice you'd gone to the Cont'nent an' I was bringin' you a bun to stop you starving.'

'This afternoon?' said Mr Marks. Beneath his professional assumption of dignity, he was an absent-minded and kind-hearted man. He had already forgotten his recent interview with William, but a moment's thought recalled it to his mind. 'Ah, yes . . . Yes, I understand . . . Well, I consider that you have dealt with me very generously, my boy. Very generously indeed . . . In similar circumstances in my own boyhood, I used to hold a court-martial and condemn the criminal to unspeakable tortures. I had a particular aversion to the science master, I remember, and I used to keep him hanging by his feet from the top of a pine tree for days on end.'

'That was a jolly good idea,' said William.

'You can have it for what it's worth,' said Mr Marks absently. He looked at his watch. 'Well, I must be going on now . . . '

'Would you like your bun, sir?' said William, taking it ou of his pocket.

Mr Marks inspected it. Despite its sojourn in William' pocket, it was comparatively clean.

'Half will be sufficient,' he said. 'Perhaps less than half.'

'I'll eat the rest,' said William, dividing the bun and dispos ing of his own share of it in two large mouthfuls.

Then he stood in the doorway and watched Mr Marks mak his way across the field to the road, eating his bun in a absent-minded, meditative fashion.

Mr James Aloysius Worfield arrived the next morning. M Marks drove him from the station in his small, battered pre war car, and later he addressed the assembled school. He wa a large stout florid man with sleek black hair and an over genial smile. In his address, which was long and rambling, h urged the virtues of 'sportsmanship' and 'cricket' and 'play ing the game' and held up Mr James Aloysius Worfield as supreme example of these virtues.

'I was a little monkey, of course,' he said, flashing hi expansive smile round the rows of bored listeners. 'I was fu of mischief, up to any prank, but I can honestly say that in a my years here I never did anything that was mean or unde hand . . . '

His audience listened with growing restiveness. Mr Mark sitting next to the orator, rested his elbow on his knees an shaded his eyes with his hand as if to conceal his feeling under an appearance of deep thought.

The applause that greeted the end of the speech was du more to relief than to any appreciation of its sentiments.

'Rotten old show-off, wasn't he?' said William to Ginger.

But Ginger wasn't interested in Mr James Aloysiu Worfield. He was only interested in Mr French.

'He's been worse than ever today,' he grumbled. 'Goin' o

n' on an' on at me. Took my caterpillar off me an' kept me in
ıt break jus' for nothin'. Well, nearly for nothin' . . . An' all
hose sarky things he kept sayin' to me. Gosh! I'm goin' to
hink of somethin' sarky to say back one of these days an' I'm
olly well goin' to say it.'

A sudden memory came to William's mind.

'Let's have a court-martial on him,' he said. 'Let's have a
:ourt-martial an' condemn him to – to unspeakable tortures.'
Ginger brightened.

'Yes, that's a good idea,' he said. 'When shall we have it?'

'We'll have it down by the river after afternoon school,'
.aid William.

They chose a secluded spot on the river-bank. A thick bush
vas chosen to represent the accused, and William and Ginger
ook up their positions facing it. William constituted himself
»resident and Ginger chief witness.

William addressed the bush sternly.

'You're a crim'nal,' he said, 'an' you've got to be punished
»y lor. Did you or did you not steal a valu'ble caterpillar from
his boy?'

The bush seemed to droop despondently.

'He did, didn't he?' said William, turning to Ginger.

'Aye, aye, sir,' said Ginger.

'You can't say "Aye, aye, sir," at a court-martial,' said
William with a touch of irritation in his voice. 'You only say
hat on ships. You say, "Yes, me lud" at a court-martial.'

'Why?' said Ginger.

'Never mind why. Say it.'

'Yes, me lud,' said Ginger.

'You stole this valu'ble caterpillar off this boy,' said
William, addressing the bush again, 'an' – an' you kept him
mprisoned in the form room when he ought to've been out in
he playground an' you— What else did he do, Ginger?'

'He called me a congenial idiot,' said Ginger.

'Gosh! That's bad!' said William, shaking his head solemnly. 'Did he use those axshul words?'

'Aye, aye, me lud,' said Ginger. 'An' he said I'd got the brains of a cheese mite an' the manners of an orang-utan.'

'Well, there's nothin' wrong with orang-utans,' said William. 'I saw one in the zoo. It acted quite sensible.'

'If you're goin' to start bein' on his side—' said Ginger hotly.

'No, I'm not, I'm not,' William assured him hastily. He assumed a ferocious scowl and addressed the bush again. 'You're a crim'nal an' you've been proved guilty of stealin valu'ble caterpillars an' keepin' boys imprisoned against th lor an' usin' bad language at them. Have you anythin' to sa in your defence?'

The bush remained silent.

'I knew you hadn't an' I jolly well wouldn't listen if yo had,' said William. 'I sentence you to—'

At this point a face appeared round the bush. It was a nar row Puck-like face, with slanting twinkling eyes, ruffle greying hair and a long humorous mouth.

'What's all this?' it said. 'A trial at law?'

'It's a court-martial,' said William coldly, 'an' it's private.

'I'm sorry for intruding,' said the man, 'but it seemed to b almost over. What is the sentence going to be?'

'Well,' said William uncertainly – for his plans had no reached beyond the actual trial – 'we might hang him by hi feet from a tree.'

'No, no,' said the man. 'Too ordinary. Let the punishmen fit the crime. He shall pick caterpillars off cabbages till no one remains in the purlieus of the village. He shall be on view in a cage at the zoo, fed on mite-infested cheese and jeered a by small boys through the bars.'

William chuckled.

'Yes, that's jolly good,' he said.

He peered around the bush in order to get a closer view of the originator of these suggestions. He saw a little man, wearing shorts and a shabby tweed jacket, sitting on the ground with a knapsack on the grass beside him.

'I was just going to have my tea,' said the man. 'Come and join me. I have a lot of food to spare because I didn't stop for lunch. Just had a beer and a hunk of bread and cheese at a pub and pushed on.'

'Thanks awfully,' said William, as the two made their way round the bush. 'That's jolly decent of you.'

'Jolly decent,' said Ginger.

'Not at all,' said the man. He opened the knapsack and took out several large packages. 'The landlady who made up my packed meal this morning had liberal notions. There should be plenty.'

There was plenty . . . sausage rolls, sandwiches, cake, apples, biscuits.

'Tuck into it,' said the man.

They tucked into it.

'Do you live here?' said William.

'No,' said the man. 'I'm doing a hiking tour. I think that October is the ideal month for hiking so I generally do one in October. This place doesn't really come into my itinerary but when I found that I was within a few miles of it, some impulse made me stretch a point and take it in. I was at school here, you see. You, I think' – he glanced at their ties – 'now attend that particular educational establishment . . . All changed since my day, I expect. I took a look at it from the outside as I passed but I didn't go in. A mistake, I always think, to revisit one's old school in any capacity. The very expression Old Boy is revolting. But when I heard your court-martial I couldn't help being interested. It brought back the memory of a court-martial we held when I was at school.' He was silent for a few moments and his lips curved into a smile. 'Quite a story, that was.'

'WE HAD A SECRET SOCIETY,' SAID THE MAN. 'WE MET
IN A CAVE NEAR MARLEIGH.'

'Tell us,' said William through a mouthful of sausage roll.
The little man leaned back and lit his pipe.

'Well, as I said, it's quite a story . . . We had a secret society.
I expect you've had a secret society.' William nodded. 'About
six of us. We all had secret names that no one else was supposed to know. All a dark secret. We met in a cave in the old
quarry near Marleigh. A cave high up on the side of the quarry
with a bush growing outside . . . A pretty stiff climb to get to
it, I can tell you. That was secret, too, of course, and we had a
lot of hocus-pocus about it. Rules and oaths of secrecy and that

sort of thing. One of the members was a boy whose secret
society name was Porky. He had small eyes and little pointed
ears like a pig. My name was Frisky, I remember, but I can't
remember why . . . An unpleasant sort of chap, Porky was, but
he threw his weight about and did a lot of smarming up to
people and somehow he took everyone in. Anyway, things
began to vanish – money from pockets, penknives and oddments from desks and lockers. So we set a watch and we
caught Porky at it . . . Have a doughnut? They look good.'

'Thanks,' said William. 'They are, too.'

'It was a bit of a shock, of course, to find that the thief was
a member of our secret society. Anyway, we had a meeting of
the society the next day, court-martialled him and told him
that he must sign a confession and we wouldn't report him to
the Head unless he started his tricks again, in which case we
would show the Head his confession. We turned him out of
the secret society, of course . . . Try one of those chocolate
biscuits.'

'Thanks,' said Ginger.

'I've tried one,' said William. 'They're jolly good. I'll try
another. What happened after that?'

The man gave a reminiscent chuckle.

'I remember Porky played one of his pleasant little tricks
on me as we were climbing out of the cave. Came up behind
me and tried to push me down the rock, but I saw him coming
and stepped aside and over he went. Crack down on a rock.
Cut his head open. Had to have half a dozen stitches in it and
was in bed for over a week. Anyway, that was the end of the
secret society.'

'Why was it the end?' said William.

'Well, the next day they started blasting in the quarry again
and blasted away all that side of it. We could see the opening
to our cave still high and dry with the bush still growing in
front, but there was no way of getting up to it. Anyway, it was

almost the end of term and we were all leaving. We were boarders and I don't suppose any of us have been near the place since. I haven't till today when I found myself a couple of miles away from it and had a sudden fancy to come over.'

'This quarry . . . ' said William thoughtfully.

'Now don't go messing about with the quarry,' said the man. 'It was dangerous enough in our day. It must be twice as dangerous now.'

'We know it . . . ' said Ginger. 'It's on the road to Marleigh, isn't it?'

'A long time ago it seems now,' said the man ruminatively. 'It was hearing your court-martial that brought it all back to my mind. Your culprit was being tried in his absence, I gather. Who was he?'

'Old Frenchie,' said William.

'Our form master,' explained Ginger.

'Well, let him have it good and proper. Don't forget. Picking caterpillars off cabbages and stuck in a cage in the zoo . . . And now you must run off or your parents will be wondering what's happened to you and I must be getting on . . . Take what's left of the food.'

'*Thanks*,' said William and Ginger simultaneously.

'An' it's all been most int'restin',' added William.

The next morning Mr French poured out his choicest sarcasms on William and Ginger, but they bore it unmoved, upheld by the pleasant vision of their tormentor laboriously removing caterpillars from cabbages and exhibiting his spindly person in a cage at the zoo.

Not only Mr French but the whole staff seemed nervy and on edge. For Mr James Aloysius Worfield was playing with Mr Marks as a cat plays with a mouse. Sometimes he seemed about to present the new pavilion and sometimes he didn't. He obviously enjoyed the sense of power that the situation gave him. He didn't know . . . He wasn't sure . . . He had seen one boy surreptitiously reading a 'comic' when he was supposed to be studying Latin verbs, and he had seen another funking his opponent's right in a boxing match. Such things were not done in his day. They weren't cricket. They weren't playing the game. They weren't keeping a straight bat. Over and over again – to anyone who would listen to him and to many who wouldn't – he described the uprightness, the manliness, the sportsmanship, the pluck that had characterised his own boyhood. He described how he had acquired the scar that ran across his forehead in defending a 'little chap' against a 'bully' who then attacked him with a 'naked penknife'.

'And I never gave him away,' he would add with his fatuous smile. 'I had my faults, of course, but I was never a sneak.'

Mr Marks wore a harassed, driven look. He was beginning to suspect that his visitor had thrown out his vague hints of a munificent 'memorial' merely in order to satisfy his self-importance and ensure his treatment as an honoured guest, without any real intention of fulfilling them. The entertainment of Mr James Aloysius Worfield was an arduous task and one of which Mr Marks and his whole staff were now heartily weary.

'Everyone's in a bad temper,' said William as he and Ginger made their way home from school. 'Thank goodness tomorrow's Saturday an' we needn't go to school.'

'Well, let's do somethin' excitin' tomorrow,' said Ginger. 'Let's play Cowboys an' Indians.'

'No, let's go an' have a look at the ole quarry,' said William. 'It sounded jolly int'restin'.'

'It sounded jolly dangerous,' said Ginger.

'Well, I'm goin' anyway,' said William, 'an' you needn't come if you don't want to.'

'Oh, I'll come,' said Ginger resignedly.

A few minutes later they stood looking at the railed-off pit from which a few jagged rocks rose precipitously.

William's eyes were fixed on a rock that rose from the farther side of the quarry. Most of the lower part had been blasted away, but a bush clung precariously to the surface near the top.

'I bet that's the cave where they used to have their secret society meetings.' he said. 'I *bet* it is. There's the bush an' you can see a sort of a little opening behind it.'

'Yes, p'raps it is,' said Ginger, his eyes following the direction of William's finger. 'Well, we've seen it so let's go back an' play Cowboys an' Indians.'

'No, I'm goin' up to have a look at it,' said William.

'Gosh! You *can't*, William,' expostulated Ginger. 'You'd never get up there. It sort of hangs out all over the rest of it. There's no way of gettin' up to it.'

'Well, I'm goin' to have a try,' said William, 'an' you needn't come if you don't want to.'

'Oh, I'll come,' said Ginger again. 'It's goin' to be the dangerousest thing we've ever done in our lives, though. I bet the birds'll be pickin' our skeletons this time tomorrow.'

But William was already making his way to the bottom of the quarry.

'Well, we got down all right,' he said, rolling the last few yards between the rocks.

'Yes,' said Ginger, picking himself out of a small pool into which his descent had led him. He looked up at the jutting ledge. It seemed higher and more inaccessible than ever. 'Gosh, William, we'll *never* do it . . . Listen. We've *seen* it. Let's – let's pretend that we've been into it.'

But William was already beginning the ascent, swinging his sturdy form from ledge to ledge with the agility of a monkey. William was surefooted and unimaginitive. Heights did not disturb him. He had supreme confidence in his own prowess. Ginger acted on the simpler method of following William in blind confidence. He used the footholds and handholds that William had used, feeling them to be endowed with some sort of magic . . . and together – miraculously, as it seemed – the two swung themselves up on to the ledge, squeezed themselves behind the bush and through the little opening.

'Gosh!' panted William, looking round. 'It's wizard, isn't it!'

The cave, despite its narrow opening, was large and roomy, stretching far back into the rock. Its advantages as a meeting place for a secret society were obvious.

William's eyes roved round it with interest. Suddenly he gave a cry of excitement.

'Look!' he said 'Here's their things!'

On a low ledge that had obviously been used as a table lay the evidence of the last meeting of the secret society before the final blasting of the quarry had cut off access to the cave. There were stubs of pencils, some mouldered remains of fruit, a dust-covered sheet of paper.

William took up the paper, blew away the dust and read:

'I, the undersigned, confess that I stole a shilling from Philips' pocket and a half a crown from Saunders' pocket and a penknife from Gregson's desk and a watch from Tillinson's locker and various other things at various times.'

The signature was 'Porky' with an indecipherable squiggle beneath it.

'Gosh! It's his confession,' he said.

'Let's bag the pencils,' said Ginger, 'an' here's quite a decent penknife. Well, it's only a *bit* rusty.'

'Here's a compass, too,' said William. 'They're jolly useful things to have, are compasses. They tell you where the North is . . . an' here's an indiarubber.' He thrust the 'confession', together with a compass and indiarubber, into his pocket.

'GOSH! IT'S HIS CONFESSION!' SAID WILLIAM.

'They don't belong to anyone now so we might as well take 'em all.'

'It's goin' to be pretty awful gettin' down again,' said Ginger, peeping out of the narrow opening and drawing quickly back.

'No, it's not,' said William. 'It's goin' to be all right. We'll get down as easy as easy.'

This, perhaps, was unduly optimistic, but after a few hair-breadth escapes they arrived, battered, bruised, cut and shaken, at the bottom of the quarry.

'Well, that was jolly int'restin',' said William, picking himself up and carelessly examining a bleeding leg. 'I'm glad we did it. I wish we'd been there in those days an' could have belonged to it.'

'An' turned out ole Porky,' chuckled Ginger, removing some loose stones from his collar. 'I'm s'prised there's any skin left on my body.'

'Let's put ole Frenchie up there the next time we court-martial him,' said William. 'I bet he'd have a job gettin' down.'

'P'raps he won't be quite so sarky on Monday after pickin' off all those caterpillars,' chuckled Ginger.

But Frenchie was even more sarky on Monday and the nerves of the whole staff were more edgy than ever. For Mr James Aloysius Worfield was still in residence, demanding constant attention, and still, apparently, he had not made up his mind about the pavilion. He was beginning to hedge even more openly, talking of the many calls on a man in his position, the erroneous idea of his wealth that seemed to have got abroad.

'I'd like to do something for the school, of course,' he said to Mr Marks. 'That is, if I were a wealthier man and had not so many commitments already.'

The state of affairs had leaked out among the pupils. A bleak drizzle of rain and a dull mist lowered further the already dejected spirits of masters and boys.

'Wish I could think of somethin' to make him give that ole pavilion an' clear off home,' said William.

'I'm sick of hearin' him talk about cricket,' said Ginger.

'Gosh! That's an idea,' said William.

'What's an idea?'

'Cricket.'

'What d'you mean, cricket?'

'Well, it's cricket he's int'rested in. Straight bats an' things. He never talks about football. It's always cricket. He's sort of got cricket on the brain . . . If he could see us playin' cricket it might put him in a good temper an' he might give the ole pavilion an' go home.'

'Cricket!' expostulated Ginger. 'You can't play cricket in October. It's pourin' with rain an' the ground's all muddy.'

William waved the objection aside.

'You can play cricket any time,' he said loftily. 'You've only got to stick stumps in the ground an' throw a ball at them. Let's get Henry an' Douglas.'

The next morning Mr James Aloysius Worfield, idly watching the boys at 'break' from the headmaster's window, was surprised to see four boys knocking stumps into the mud-swamped ground and proceeding to engage in what was evidently intended to be a game of cricket. He went down to investigate. He approached the players at the bottom of the playground. Ginger stood before the wicket, displaying an elaborately straight bat. William was preparing to bowl. Henry and Douglas stood in the attitude of expectant fielders.

'What on earth—?' began Mr Worfield.

William delivered the ball.

He slipped in the mud in the act of delivering it and fell headlong.

The ball soared through the air and landed neatly on Mr Worfield's brow.

Mr Worfield in his turn staggered backwards, slipped in the mud and fell headlong.

A titter arose from the watching boys.

Purple with rage, Mr Worfield seized William by the collar and dragged him indoors to the headmaster's study.

'This boy,' he sputtered, 'has had the audacity to throw a ball at me. Deliberately throw a ball at me. I demand that he shall be instantly and severely punished.'

Mr Marks looked at William's mud-covered countenance.

'I can't even see which boy it is,' he said. 'Wipe the mud off your face, boy.'

William delved into his pocket. He knew that somewhere

beneath the accumulation of odds and ends there was a handkerchief. He found it and drew it out. The accumulation of odds and ends fell upon the carpet, among them a crumpled piece of paper with the words 'I, the undersigned . . . ' and the signature 'Porky' plainly visible.

Mr Worfield's eyes rested on it and a curious change took place in his countenance. The ruddy colour left his cheeks and an ashen hue invaded them. His eyes, fixed on the paper, bulged and grew bloodshot.

'Pick up that rubbish,' said Mr Marks.

William picked up that rubbish. His gaze was fixed on Mr Worfield.

Emotion had emphasised the peculiarities of Mr Worfield's features – the small eyes, the pointed ears, the thick nose that resembled a snout. The jagged scar across his brow showed up sharply.

'Porky!' gasped William.

Mr Marks looked at William in amazement and then, with increasing amazement, at Mr Worfield. Beads of perspiration stood out on Mr Worfield's brow and trickled down his face. His pallid lips were drawn back in a sickly smile.

'Come, come, come!' he said. 'Perhaps I was over hasty. Doubtless I was over hasty. I'm a hasty man. Impulsive, generous, courageous – but inclined to be hasty.' He took out his handkerchief and wiped the perspiration from his brow. 'Let me have a word with this boy alone, Headmaster.'

Mr Marks shrugged his shoulders and left the room.

Mr Worfield turned to William. The perspiration still glistened on his brow. The sickly smile was still plastered on his lips.

'Where did you find that piece of paper, my boy?' he said. 'The one that fell out of your pocket?'

'Oh, that!' said William. 'I found it in a cave in the old quarry.'

Mr Worfield uttered a neighing sound that was evidently intended to be a laugh.

'I remember. I remember . . . Some boys held secret society meetings up there. I wasn't a member myself, but I heard about it. I – er—'

A sudden idea had occurred to William. That indecipherable squiggle after the name 'Porky' . . . He took out the paper and examined it . . . It wasn't quite indecipherable, after all. Though hastily written and almost illegible, it still represented the words James Aloysius Worfield.

'It's got your name after "Porky",' he said. 'It's got James Aloysius Worfield.'

Mr Worfield made a movement towards William. William made a movement towards the door, slipping the paper into his pocket. Mr Worfield stood, reconsidering his tactics. The boy, though thickset, looked active and nimble. He would dodge round the furniture. He would dart out of the door. The whole thing would be in the open. Again he uttered the neighing sound.

'Yes, yes,' he said. 'I remember. We had a sort of game. We all wrote imaginary confessions. How it all comes back! One wet afternoon . . . I've forgotten what I pretended I'd done . . . Now you're a sensible boy. Let's do a deal. This bit of paper is of no use to you, but it will be of value to me – just as a little memento of my boyhood. It's useless to you, isn't it?'

William's school reports emphasised with monotonous regularity his lack of serious application to his studies, but he was not altogether devoid of intelligence. He turned a bland, expressionless face to his interlocutor.

'I think Mr Marks'd sort of like it, too,' he said. 'He's got a sort of museum of old things about the school. I think he'd like this for his museum.'

Mr Worfield moistened his dry lips.

'What nonsense!' he said. 'A mere paper game! What

WILLIAM EXAMINED THE PAPER, 'IT'S GOT YOUR NAME
AFTER "PORKY",' HE SAID.

possible interest could it have for him? A paper game of imaginary confessions played on a wet afternoon.'

'But Frisky said . . . '

A greenish hue spread over Mr Worfield's face.

'You know Frisky?' he stammered.

'Oh, yes. I know Frisky,' said William.

Mr Worfield abandoned finesse.

'How much will you take for it?' he said.

'Well,' said William thoughtfully, 'Mr Marks sort of wants a pavilion for the playing field.'

'Of course, of course, my boy,' said Mr Worfield, recovering something of his aplomb. 'I have every intention of giving one. That was one of my main objects in coming here.'

'Shower-baths and changing rooms.'

'Of course, of course.'

William thought quickly.

'A holiday tomorrow.'

'Yes, yes, my boy,' said Mr Worfield with the ghost of his old geniality. 'All work and no play makes Jack a dull boy. Ha-ha!'

'An' me not gettin' in a row over that cricket ball, 'cause we thought you'd like it. Straight bats an' things.'

Mr Worfield flinched.

'Exactly, exactly. Boys will be boys. I was one myself once. Ha-ha! And – er – I take it that this foolish little paper game will go no further? I mean, there might be people who wouldn't realise that it was only a game.'

'Yes, that's all right,' said William. 'I forget things jolly quick.'

Mr Worfield met William's eye and somehow felt that he could trust him.

'Well . . . ' he said, holding out his hand.

William placed his hand firmly over his pocket.

'Things are in a bit of a muddle in my pocket,' he said. 'I'll be gettin' 'em sorted out while you fix it up with Mr Marks.'

Mr Worfield threw him a glance of unwilling admiration as he went to the door.

Mr Marks and Mr French were talking together at the end of the corridor.

'Come along, Headmaster,' called Mr Worfield. 'Our little interview is over.'

Mr Marks looked curiously at his guest as he entered the study, followed by Mr French. He was a strange and not pre-possessing spectacle. Red and green patches seemed to alter-nate on his face, his brow was still damp with perspiration and his thick lips were twitching nervously.

'Well, well, well,' he said, baring his teeth in a wolfish grin, 'we've had our little talk and I'm willing to overlook the whole thing . . . I – I ask that the boy has no further punish-ment.'

'As you wish,' said Mr Marks.

'Your lucky day, Brown,' said Mr French dryly.

Mr Worfield took out his watch.

'I'm afraid that I must return this evening and I'd like to fix up that little affair of the pavilion with you, Headmaster, before I go.'

He drew a cheque-book from his pocket and went to the desk. Mr Marks and Mr French followed him, staring with amazement at the figures he was writing on the cheque.

'It's extremely generous of you, Worfield,' said Mr Marks. 'I'm most grateful.'

'Not at all, not at all,' said Mr Worfield. 'That should cover all incidentals such as changing-rooms, etcetera.'

Then they turned to William, who stood watching them impassively.

'What are you hanging about for, Brown?' said Mr Marks, slipping the cheque into his wallet. 'Off with you!'

'What on earth has the boy got in his pockets?' said Mr

Worfield, neighing on a high-pitched note. 'Turn them out, boy . . . String, 'bus tickets, matchbox, bit of paper . . . The fire's the best place for all that junk.'

He threw the handful on to the flames, watched his 'confession' blacken into ashes, then drew a deep breath and mopped his brow again.

'G'bye,' said William politely as he turned to the door.

Ginger was waiting for him at the gate.

'Told you it wouldn't work,' he said gloomily. 'What happened?'

'Oh, nothin' much,' said William vaguely. 'A bit of a mess-up but it ended all right. An' I've got some good news.'

'What?'

'There's goin' to be a holiday tomorrow. A whole holiday.'

'Good!' said Ginger. 'Let's play Cowboys and Indians.'

Mr Marks and Mr French stood by the window, looking at the taxi that was bearing their guest down the drive on its way to the station.

As it vanished from sight Mr Marks took the cheque from his pocket and contemplated it with satisfaction.

'Well, we got it,' he said.

'We got it,' said Mr French, 'in spite of young Brown.'

'In spite of young Brown,' agreed Mr Marks. Then a thoughtful look came over his face. 'Or could it be – we shall never know, of course – could it possibly be *because* of young Brown?'

Chapter 7

A Helping Hand for Ethel

'I want to do somethin' for Ethel,' said William, kicking a stone from one side of the road to the other.

'Why?' said Ginger, neatly stopping the stone with his foot and returning it.

'She never does anythin' for you,' said Douglas.

'I thought you thought she was awful,' said Henry.

'Oh, yes, she *is* awful,' said William, 'but all girls are awful, an' anyway other people's sisters aren't any worse than what she is.'

'Yes, but why do you want to *do* somethin' for her?' said Ginger.

'Well, you see,' said William, 'she gave me her old fountain pen las' week an' only half the nib was broke an' yesterday my mother was talkin' to me about givin' people a helpin' hand an' not always thinkin' about yourself an' it started me wonderin' who to give a helpin' hand to an' I sort of fixed on Ethel.'

The Outlaws' expressions showed disapproval not unmixed with apprehension.

'Well, I still don't see why you've got to fix on Ethel,' said Ginger. 'I should've thought she was the last person in the world that *wanted* a helpin' hand.'

'We'll get in a muddle the minute we start,' said Douglas gloomily.

'Thought you thought she was mean an' stuck-up an' disagreeable,' said Henry.

'Yes, I do,' said William. 'I never said I didn't, but I don't know anyone else's sister that isn't. Anyway, I've sort of fixed on her an' I'm not goin' to start unfixin' now.'

'If you want someone to give a helpin' hand to,' said Henry, 'there's me. I've always wanted that water-pistol of yours. It holds more water than mine does.'

'Well, I'm jolly well not goin' to give it to you,' said William with spirit. 'I'm not goin' to give anythin' to anyone. I'm only givin' a helpin' hand an' a helpin' hand's different from a water-pistol.'

'Well, how are you goin' to give her a helpin' hand?'

'I've been thinkin' about that. At first I thought I'd paper her bedroom for her for a surprise – she said she wanted it papered, an' there's some old paper in the box-room – an' then I remembered that I'd got in a bit of a mess the las' time I tried paperin' a room, so I thought I'd p'raps better not. Then I thought I'd paint her chest of drawers blue 'cause she's said that Peggy Barton had got hers painted blue an' it looked nice, then I remembered that paint's got a sort of way of spreading over everything else, an', anyway, I haven't got any blue paint an' I'm not goin' to waste money buyin' it – even if I had any money an' I haven't – so I thought I wouldn't do that either.'

'Well, what *are* you goin' to do?' said Henry.

'I've got a jolly good idea,' said William complacently. 'Listen. She was talkin' to Mother las' night an' she said she was sick of her job an' wanted another, so' – simply – 'I thought I'd get her another job.'

They gazed at him in silent amazement. Ginger was the first to find his voice.

'Gosh, William, you *can't*. Not a *job*. Not for a grown-up person.'

'Why not?' said William airily. 'I bet I can easy. There mus' be hundreds an' thousands of jobs about an' I bet I can find jus' one for one person.'

'What sort of job?' said Douglas. 'Don't get her servin' in Marleigh sweet shop. The woman that's there now puts one on after the scales have gone down an' I bet Ethel wouldn't do that.'

'No,' agreed William with a touch of bitterness, 'she'd be more likely to take one off. No, I won't get her in a sweet shop. I'll get her in somethin' a bit more excitin' than that. I don't s'pose she'd call it a helpin' hand, either, gettin' her in a sweet shop. She says that lollipops are disgusting an' she says that the sight of sugar mice makes her feel sick, an' she doesn't even like liqu'rice bootlaces.'

'Well, don't get her teachin' in our school,' said Douglas anxiously. 'There's enough bad-tempered people teachin' in our school.'

'No, I'm not goin' to get her to teach,' William reassured him. 'She couldn't teach, anyway. She doesn't know any-thin'.'

'Well, what sort of a job *are* you goin' to get her?' said Henry a little impatiently.

'Well, I've been thinkin',' said William. 'She'd make a jolly good spy. She's the nosiest person I've ever come across an' she's got red hair. I've read lots of tales about women spies an' they've all got red hair.'

The Outlaws considered this in silence.

'Yes, but you can't get a person a job as a spy,' said Ginger at last.

'I don't see why not,' said William. 'There mus' be ways of gettin' people jobs as spies. I mean, people *are* spies, so there mus' be ways of gettin' them to be.'

'How are you goin' to start?' said Henry.

'Well, I have sort of started,' said William, 'but axshully I didn't get very far. I went into Hadley with my mother this mornin' 'cause she wanted to get me a pair of shoes an' while she was payin' for them I jus' slipped into the Labour

Exchange 'cause it was nex' to the shoe shop an' I asked them if they'd got any jobs as spies. Gosh! They were mad. I thought the man was goin' to jump over the counter an' murder me. I bet' – darkly – 'they're jus' a gang of spies themselves. They'd got a sort of suspicious look about them an' there was a funny sort of thing in the shape of a stove with smoke coming out. They pretended it was an ordin'ry stove that wasn't working prop'ly, but I bet they're makin' atomic bombs. I've a good mind to set the p'lice on them.'

'Well, anyway, you can't go on with the spy idea,' said Henry, bringing him back to the subject in hand.

'N-not jus' at the moment,' agreed William regretfully, 'but it's the one I like best an' I'm goin' to sort of keep it in my mind. It'd jus' suit her. She could be as nosey as she liked an' get paid for it.'

'Well, what other ideas have you got?' said Ginger, who was becoming interested despite himself.

'I think she'd make a jolly good film star,' said William. 'She's got a face like a film star . . . At least' – he hastened to qualify his statement – 'it seems an awful face to me, but people that don't know her as well as what I do make a fuss about it. Archie Mannister writes po'ms to it.'

'She'd have to act as well as look like what she does,' said Henry.

'Yes, but she can act all right,' said William. 'She acted in that play the tennis club did an' you could hear every single word she said till they all started giggling 'cause one of them fell over the mat an' after that they were all giggling so much that you couldn't hear what any of them said, but she mus' be a good actress 'cause someone gave her a great bunch of roses at the end. I bet it wouldn't matter if she started gigglin' on the films 'cause if it was a funny film it'd fit in with it an' if it was a sad one it'd cheer people up that don't like sad ones.'

'Yes, but how're you goin' to get her on the films?' said Henry.

'It *is* goin' to end in a muddle,' said Douglas with simple conviction.

'Well, I've not quite made up my mind about that,' said William. 'I think I'll have to wait till I meet someone on the films.'

'An' you're not likely to do *that*,' said Ginger.

'How d'you know I'm not?' challenged William. 'All sorts of people meet all sorts of people every day, don't they? Well, it's news to *me* if they don't. It's news to *me* if all sorts of people don't meet all sorts of people every day. Any person's jus' as likely to meet any other person as not. A film man might be jus' comin' along the road now. We might meet him jus' when we get round that corner. Listen! I can hear footsteps an' I bet it's a film man.'

A tense silence fell over them as they approached the bend in the road, but no more exciting apparition met their eyes than Mr Monks, the Vicar. He was surprised to find the four boys staring at him, open-mouthed, as he came round the corner.

'Good-morning, boys,' he said briskly and passed on.

Turning round after a few paces, he found them still standing there, gazing after him in a spell-bound fashion.

'Tut, tut!' he muttered. 'Dear, dear! Up to some mischief, I'll be bound.'

'Well, it wasn't a film man,' said Ginger, as the four began to resume their way.

'No, but it might have been,' said William in the triumphant tone of one who has proved his point. 'I said it might have been an' it *might*. The nex' time we go round a corner it prob'ly will be.'

'Yes, but we can't spend the rest of our lives goin' round an' round corners, 'case we meet a film man,' said Ginger.

'No, I know we can't,' said William. 'I'm not s'gestin' we do. Anyway, I've got to get this job for Ethel pretty quick, so I'm not goin' to waste any more time on spies or film stars. I'm goin' to think out somethin' else.'

'There's advertisements in newspapers about jobs,' said Henry. 'That's where people get 'em.'

'Yes, that's a good idea,' said William. 'Let's do that. Let's go home now – 'cause it's lunch-time, anyway – an' find some newspapers an' bring them to the old barn this afternoon.'

The four met in the old barn immediately after lunch, armed with such newspapers and magazines as they had been able to collect from their various households – Ginger, having been unable to find one, had unceremoniously dismembered the fire that his mother's char had carefully 'laid' a few minutes before. William was accompanied by Jumble, who pranced in at his heels with his usual air of joyous irresponsibility and set to work promptly and thoroughly on any stray newspapers that came his way.

William sorted out the newspapers with a sternly judicial air.

'Poultry magazines aren't any good,' he said, throwing the *Poultry World* on to one side, where Jumble seized it, tossed it into the air, then chased it furiously round the barn. 'She doesn't like hens, anyway. She says they've got mean faces. I bet *she'd* be pretty mean to 'em too if she had to look after them . . . This *Rabbit Fancier*'s no good either.' Jumble sprang upon the *Rabbit Fancier*, tore it limb from limb, swallowed half the front cover, played hide-and-seek with the rest, then returned with a threatening growl to deal with the scattered remnants of the *Poultry World*. 'She doesn't like rabbits either. I had one once and she said it ground its teeth at her . . . *Review of Public Affairs* . . . What's that about?'

' "GOOD PLAIN COOK WANTED", ' READ WILLIAM. 'WELL,
I DUNNO ABOUT THAT . . . '

'Pol'tics,' said Henry.

'Well, that's no good either, then. She doesn't like pol'tics.
She once met a Member of Parliament that was so ign'rant he
didn't know Stewart Granger from Clark Gable, an' she said
it put her off pol'tics for the rest of her life.'

He was left finally with a copy of the *Hadley Advertiser*
and a selection of the morning and evening papers. He spread
the *Hadley Advertiser* on the ground and the four of them lay
on their stomachs in a row studying the 'Situations Vacant'
column, while Jumble left his paper-chase to push an enquir-
ing nose between William and Ginger.

' "Good plain cook wanted," ' read William. 'Well, I dunno
about that . . . '

'Is she a good cook?' said Ginger.

'Yes, she is. She made a cake las' Saturday an' it was only
a bit burned at the bottom an' a bit sort of sunk in at the top.
They gave it to me an' it was jolly good, but she's not plain,
so that one won't do . . . Here's another for a cook . . . No,
that's got to be plain, too . . . '

'Why do they all want cooks plain?' said Douglas with a
mystified expression.

'Dunno,' said William. 'Take your nose out of the way,

Jumble . . . Look! This one might do. "Wanted companion-help. Able to drive car". I bet she wouldn't be much help, but she can drive a car . . . No. Look! It goes on, "Must be careful driver". She wouldn't do for that. She's an awful driver. She nearly ran over a p'liceman las' week. He was mad at first, then she started smilin' at him an' he stopped bein' mad . . . Hi! Leave that paper alone, Jumble.'

'Could you get her a job smilin' at p'licemen for people that have car accidents?' suggested Ginger tentatively.

'Sort of hire her out to criminals at so much a time,' said Douglas, developing the theme.

'Gosh, no!' said William. 'She's jolly bad-tempered some days. There's days when she snaps your head off for nothin' at all – jus' 'cause you've borrowed her lipstick for a Red Indian game, or somethin' like that.'

'What's she good at?' said Henry. 'I mean, if we're goin' to get her a job, we ought to think what she's good at.'

'She's a jolly good runner,' said William with a certain grudging admiration in his voice. 'She used to win all the races when she was at school.'

'We might get her a job in the Olympic Games,' said Henry thoughtfully, 'but they're only held every four years, so we'd have to get her jobs for all the years in between an' it might be difficult.'

'Look! Here's another,' said Ginger. ' "Gentlewoman wanted as companion-help to elderly lady. No rough work. Every comfort".'

'Yes, that sounds all right,' said William, interested. 'She's jolly good at havin' every comfort . . . No, it won't do. Look! It says "Pleasant disposition essential" an' she's jolly well not got one. I bet she'd snap this elderly lady's head off the minute she started crackin' nuts or chewin' gum or borrowing her things . . . No, she wouldn't do for that.'

'Here's another,' said Henry. 'It's for a cook-housekeeper

an' they don't seem to mind about her bein' pretty. It doesn't say "plain," anyway. It says, "Quiet family. No late hours".'

'Gosh, that wouldn't suit her,' said William. 'She doesn't like quiet fam'lies an' she likes late hours. She didn't come in till two o'clock from the tennis club dance.'

'Look! Here's another. "Wanted, companion-help under thirty—"'

'That's all right,' said William. 'She's under thirty.'

'"Must be devoted to animals, especially cats".'

'She can't bear cats,' said William.

'That's a pity,' said Henry, ''cause it's jus' over at Marleigh. We could've gone an' got it all fixed up for her, if she'd liked cats.'

'Well, she likes *some* animals,' said William. 'P'raps we could get 'em to change.'

'What sort does she like?' said Ginger.

'She likes those big dogs called wolf-hounds, 'cause some-one once took a photo of her standing with a soppy sort of look on her face an' her hand on its head an' she was so pleased with it she got it made into a Christmas card an' put on no end of side about it. She's always goin' on at poor ole Jumble 'cause he's not a wolf-hound. Axshully he's got a bit of wolf-hound in him, but she won't see it.'

'They might change,' said Ginger, ' – the people that adver-tised, I mean – if we could make 'em see that wolf-hounds were better than cats.'

'Well, they jolly well are,' said William. 'They guard the house an' cats haven't even the sense to do that.'

'No, they haven't,' agreed Ginger. 'My aunt had a cat and it let a burglar come in the middle of the night and walk off with all her things.'

'They can't bark,' said Douglas in extenuation.

'No, but they can mew,' said Ginger, 'an' this one didn't even do that.'

'They look after babies, too, do wolf-hounds,' said Henry. 'There's a tale about a wolf-hound that was left to look after a baby—'

'A dog sitter-in?' said Douglas. 'Gosh! That's a jolly good idea.'

'Anyway, it killed a wolf that was killin' the baby it was lookin' after and then it got killed by a man.'

'That's a silly tale,' said William, 'but it's a good idea – dog sitters-in. We'll tell her about that. We'll 'splain that dogs guard houses an' mind babies an' cats don't do anythin' but sit about drinkin' milk.'

'If she had a lot of dogs she could let 'em out sittin'-in with babies,' said Henry, 'an' she'd make a lot of money an' they'd catch burglars an' – an' anyway a dog's fun an' a cat isn't.'

'An' Ethel could have a jolly good time with them,' said Ginger. 'She could have her hand on a different one's head every day.'

'I bet *they'd* get a bit sick of it,' said William. 'Anyway, baby sitters-in get about two shillin's a night, so if she had six dogs an' trained 'em prop'ly—'

'But there aren't any wolves round here for them to kill,' said Douglas.

'They needn't kill wolves, you chump,' said William. 'They can jus' sit on the hearth-rug an' watch the baby. I bet you could train 'em to do that easy.' He looked at Jumble, who was hard at work on the Parish Magazine that had been Douglas's sole contribution. 'I've a good mind to train Jumble for it. It'd be jolly useful to get two shillin's a night. Trouble with Jumble is, he always wants to play with babies an' he's got a way of chewin' up eiderdowns an' pillows, but I bet I could get him out of it.'

'Well, about this job for Ethel,' said Ginger. 'Where does this cat person live?'

They studied the paper again.

'Here it is. "Miss Tufton, Acacia Villa, Marleigh".'

'Come on,' said William, rising to his feet. 'Let's go there . . . P'raps we'd better take Jumble home first. He might make a muddle of it.'

'Seems to me it's in a pretty good muddle to start with,' said Douglas.

'Don't be an idiot,' said William. 'It's a jolly good plan an' it's as simple as simple.'

'Sounds complicated enough to me,' said Douglas. 'All spies an' film stars an' dog sitters-in an' wolves killin' babies an'—'

'Oh, shut up,' said William. 'All plans sound complicated at first, an' then they start workin' out all right. At least' – after a moment's thought – 'some do, an' I bet this will . . . Where's Jumble?'

But Jumble, having realised that William intended to exclude him from the adventure, was already halfway across the field in the direction of Marleigh.

'Oh, well, I don't 'spect he'll do any harm,' said William. 'He might show this woman that dogs are better than cats. He might show her that dogs guard houses and mind babies an'—' He looked vaguely round. 'Pity we can't find a baby to take along an' show her prop'ly . . . '

'Oh, come on,' said Douglas. 'We don't want it any more complicated than what it is already. We had enough baby-mindin' with that baby at The Hawthorns.'

The four walked across the field to join the Marleigh road, where Jumble was waiting for them, waving his tail in mingled triumph and apology.

'He's jolly clever,' said William proudly. 'He didn't want to be shut up at home, 'cause he wanted to help us get this job for Ethel. There isn't a cat in the world would have thought of that.'

'I wonder where this house is,' said Douglas apprehensively.

'We'd better make up our minds what we're goin' to say when we get there.'

'There's no need for that,' said William with a nonchalant air. 'We'll sort of lead up to it by a bit of p'lite conversation same as grown-ups do, then we'll jus' tell her we want the job for Ethel, only we want wolf-hounds 'stead of cats. Once she re'lises that wolf-hounds are better than cats, I bet she'll change them. It's quite simple.'

But they slowed their pace a little as they approached the small neat detached house that bore the name Acacia Villa. Even Jumble seemed to be assailed by secret doubts, falling behind them and appearing to concentrate his whole attention on an old tin that he found in the ditch, pushing it along with his nose, making sudden rushes at it from the cover of a tuft of grass.

The Outlaws stood clustered at the gate of the villa.

'Come on,' said William at last, speaking in a deep hoarse voice and walking up to the front door.

There he raised the knocker and beat a tattoo of a dozen loud knocks, partly in order to emphasise the importance of his mission and partly because that was his usual way of announcing his presence at people's front doors. Douglas had slipped to the rear of the group.

'I still think we ought to've thought out somethin' def'nite to say,' he said. 'I think we ought to've *organised* it more.'

'Don't be silly,' said William. 'We've got it all thought out. I'll put on my p'lite manner an' we'll make a bit of p'lite conversation then we'll ask for this job for Ethel an' 'splain about the cats. I've got it all organised im my mind. I'm a jolly good organist.'

'Organiser,' murmured Henry.

'She can only say "no," anyway,' said Ginger.

'I've known people do more than that,' said Douglas darkly.

They stood for a moment in silence, looking with set strained expressions at the closed door.

'I bet she's not heard,' said William. 'I'll knock a bit louder.'

'If she's out,' said Douglas, the anxiety of his face lightening somewhat, 'we'd better give it up. We'll have done our best.'

'We could try the one with every comfort,' said Ginger.

William raised the knocker and beat a second resounding tattoo on the door.

'I bet she's out,' said Douglas, turning hopefully towards the gate.

Suddenly the door opened and a middle-aged woman with grey hair and a thin vague-looking face stood looking at them.

'Are you trying to break the house down?' she said sternly.

'No,' William reassured her. 'No, we're not tryin' to break the house down.' He assumed the wooden expression and glassy smile of his 'polite manner' and added, 'Good afternoon.'

'I was down at the bottom of the garden,' said the woman, ignoring his greeting, 'and I came as soon as I could.' She examined a small pane of glass in the door. 'It's a mercy every piece of glass in the place isn't broken. Is that the way you generally knock at people's doors?'

'Yes,' said William simply, then, intensifying the glassiness of his smile, added, 'How are you?'

'What do you mean, how am I?' said the woman. 'I've not been ill.'

'I'm glad you haven't been ill,' said William, baring his teeth with a further effort. 'It's a nice day, isn't it?'

The woman stared at him and he abandoned his smile to give his followers a scowl that urged them to second his efforts.

'The days are drawing in,' said Henry hastily, repeating a

remark that he had overheard in the post-office the day before.

'An' the nights are drawing out,' said Ginger after a moment's thought.

They looked at Douglas, who turned purple with mental effort as he strove to find some suitable contribution.

'The evenings,' he said at last, 'seem pretty much the same,' then, with a burst of inspiration, repeated a remark that he had heard his father make at breakfast, 'an' our foreign affairs seem to have reached a deadlock.'

'That's a silly thing to say,' said Ginger.

'It's as sens'ble as what you said.'

'It isn't.'

'It is.'

'It isn't.'

'It is. Anyway, I heard a grown-up say mine.'

'An' I heard a grown-up say mine.'

'Shut up,' said William sternly. 'Can't you make p'lite conversation for two minutes without quarrelling over it?'

Amazement and indignation had been struggling for the mastery on Miss Tufton's face, and now indignation won.

'If you've come here to be impertinent—' she said.

'No, we haven't,' protested William, hastily assuming his glassy smile again and stretching it to its utmost length. 'We only thought we'd better do a bit of p'lite conversation first, same as grown-ups do, but we've really come about that job.'

'Job?' said Miss Tufton.

'Yes. The companion-help, devoted to cats.'

The severity of Miss Tufton's face softened.

'So you little fellows are devoted to cats and want to help me look after my pussies. But I'm afraid I don't want four little boys. I want one girl.'

'Yes, I know,' said William. 'That's what we've come

about. About a girl. We've got one. A girl, I mean. We've got a girl to be your companion-help.'

Bewilderment returned again to Miss Tufton's small neat face. She gazed around.

'But where is she?'

'She's not here,' said William. 'She doesn't know about it yet. I mean, we're gettin' it for a sort of surprise for her. A sort of helpin' hand.'

'Now run away, children,' said Miss Tufton. 'I haven't time to play games with you this morning. I'm glad you like pussies, but—'

'Yes, but listen,' said William breathlessly. 'This girl's my sister an' she's all right. 'Least, she's all right when she's in a good temper an' she's a jolly good runner, but there aren't any jobs for runners, an' she can cook but she's not plain, an' she's devoted to animals but they've got to be a special sort an'—'

Miss Tufton raised a hand to stem the torrent of William's eloquence.

'You mean your sister wants this job?' she said.

'Y-yes,' said William, frowning thoughtfully. 'At least we've come to see about it for her 'cause of those special sort of animals that she's devoted to.' He realised suddenly that their hostess was keeping them standing on her doorstep and a note of severity crept into his voice. 'We'll come in an' sit down if you like. We'll wipe our shoes.'

Suiting the action to the words, he entered the hall, followed by the other three, and began to wipe his shoes on the mat. The four crowded together, scraping their shoes on the mat with a thoroughness and concentration of purpose suggestive of some ritual dance.

Miss Tufton watched them helplessly. She was a little deaf and had not been able to understand much of what they said, but she gathered that they were four young cat-lovers who had called on her because they were attracted by the mention of cats in her advertisement. For some time she had had in her mind a vague plan of organising a League of Cat Lovers among the children of the neighbourhood, and these, she thought, might form the nucleus of it.

'Well, come in and see my pussies,' she said, opening a door and ushering them into a little room where six cats sat round the fire and as many more about the room on chairs and settee. 'Aren't they lovely!'

'They're all right as *cats*,' said William slowly.

'Yes, dear. So affectionate, so sweet, so – so trusting, aren't they?'

'They don't mind babies,' said Ginger.

'No, dear. They don't mind anyone who's kind to them.'

'I mean—' began Ginger, but Douglas interrupted him.

'That tale where the wolf bit the baby an' the dog bit the wolf couldn't have happened with cats.'

'No, dear,' said Miss Tufton vaguely. 'Properly treated, cats are the gentlest creatures in the world. Now if you boys would form—'

'Jus' drinkin' milk,' said Henry. 'There's nothin' to it.'

'You're quite right, dear,' said Miss Tufton. 'They're no trouble at all to feed. Just a little milk and, perhaps, a little fish. Now if you boys would form the nucleus—'

'But listen,' said Ginger. 'When this burglar came to my aunt's house her cat didn't even mew. It jus' stayed quiet.'

'I know, dear,' said Miss Tufton with a fond smile. 'So calm, so detached, so philosophical. I do so agree that that's part of their charm.'

'But a dog would have barked,' said Ginger.

'Yes,' agreed Miss Tufton. 'Noisy creatures!'

They stared at her.

'But listen,' said William. 'If you had wolf-hounds 'stead of cats, you'd – you'd like 'em better. You don't know what they're like 'cause you've never tried 'em. I've got a dog. He's not a wolf-hound, but—'

At that moment, Jumble entered. He entered like a whirlwind, flinging himself in tempestuous delight on this roomful of his natural foes. He had chased cats in ones or twos or even threes, but never before had Fate delivered a whole roomful into his hands. It was one of the most exhilarating moments of his life. The room was filled with a plunging, scratching barking, miaouing medley of cats and Jumble.

Miss Tufton screamed. Two cats streaked up the curtain and brought down the whole contraption – rod and all. One jumped on to the top of the piano, scattering china ornaments and photographs in all directions. A mangy grey warrior scratched Jumble's face. Another jumped on to his back. Jumble freed himself and made a dash at the coal-box beneath which a rusty semi-Persian had taken refuge, sending coal and semi-Persian hurtling over the hearth-rug. Miss Tufton seized a poker and began to chase the flying tornado of cats and Jumble round the room. William, surveying the scene in frozen horror and deciding that flight was the only possible solution of the problem, turned to the door.

'Come on!' he said tersely, and the four fled down the path to the road and across the fields, not stopping till they reached the safety of William's garden.

'Well, that *proves* it, doesn't it?' panted William, as they closed the gate behind them. 'That couldn't have happened with wolf-hounds.'

'Well, it's messed *that* up all right,' said Henry.

'Hope Jumble gets back alive,' said Ginger.

'*Course* he will,' said William. 'A few cats are nothin' to Jumble.'

And a few cats were nothing to Jumble. He came rollicking down the road a minute or two later with a bleeding nose, a torn ear and an air of jaunty triumph, throwing himself

JUMBLE ENTERED LIKE A WHIRLWIND AND FLUNG HIMSELF
ON HIS NATURAL FOES. MISS TUFTON SCREAMED.

exuberantly upon William as if congratulating him on their victory.

'Good ole Jumble!' said William. 'He was only tryin' to help. He thought if he cleared out those cats she'd have to get wolf-hounds. It was jolly clever of him.'

'Well, you'll have to give up that idea of findin' a job for Ethel now,' said Douglas. 'I said it'd get us into a muddle.'

'Yes, I s'pose I will,' said William regretfully. 'There doesn't seem anythin' else we can do.'

But the next day he heard that Marleigh Manor had been rented for the summer by a Mr Adolph Klein, the head of one of the lesser known film companies, and his interest in the subject revived.

'I said all along she'd make a jolly good film star,' he said. 'She'd make a better film star than she'd make a companion to cats – or even wolf-hounds, come to that. It's a jolly good thing Jumble messed up that cat plan – I always said he was jolly clever – 'cause now we can get on with that film star plan.'

'You can't jus' get a person to be a film star in a minute,' said Ginger. 'I bet they've got to have a special trainin' an' pass exams an' things.'

'No, I don't think so,' said Henry. 'I think they've jus' got to have long eyelashes an' special sort of teeth an' be able to act.'

'Well, she ought to be all right, then,' said William. 'She's always puttin' black stuff on her eyelashes an' she went to the dentist las' week an' she can act all right when she's not gigglin'. I bet he gives her a job.'

'But they're high up, are film people,' said Douglas. 'You won't even get a chance to speak to him.'

'I bet I will,' said William. 'I bet I get a chance to speak to him before the end of the week.'

And William did get a chance to speak to him before the end of the week.

Mr Adolph Klein, having been ordered a complete rest and country air by his doctor, had taken Marleigh Manor because it was a large house with a large garden and Mr Adolph Klein liked to do things in a large way. But already he was becoming bored. He was tired of the house, the garden and such society as the place afforded. Mr Adolph Klein's sole subject of conversation was Mr Adolph Klein, and no one in this benighted place seemed to be interested in it. All they seemed to be interested in was the weather, their gardens, the Flower Show, and the prospects of the harvest. No one here had even heard of his last film, and, what was worse, no one seemed to want to hear about it.

So that it was not perhaps surprising that, as he was idly strolling across the field one morning, a gleam of interest came into his face at a sight that would normally not have interested him at all – the sight of a scruffy small boy with upstanding hair and downsliding socks sitting on the bottom step of the stile, his chin in his hands, gazing into the distance.

'Good-morning, my child,' said Mr Adolph Klein graciously.

William looked up, and his mouth dropped open in amazement as his eyes fell on the large flashily-dressed figure, with the prominent nose, short-sighted eyes – framed in enormous horn-rims – and lips pursed over a huge cigar. He had been sitting there for the last ten minutes trying to devise some way of getting into touch with the film magnate, and here before him stood the film magnate himself.

'Gosh!' he said.

Mr Klein, feeling flattered by the tone, smiled benignly.

'Are you – are you the film man?' said William.

Mr Klein, who was unaccustomed to exercise and was feeling a little out of breath, sat down on the top rung of the stile, removed the cigar from his mouth, and twirled a silver-mounted stick.

'I am Adolph Klein,' he said with simple dignity, 'of the Adolph Klein film company.'

'You – you – you axshully make films?' said William, who still couldn't believe that Fate had come to his help so promptly.

'I make films, my child,' said Mr Klein. He gave William a pitying smile as he added, 'Without the Adolph Klein films, the film industry could hardly be said to exist.'

'*Gosh!*' said William. 'An' – an' – an' can you get people jobs on the films?'

'I *am* the films,' said Mr Klein with such a sweeping flourish of his walking-stick that he nearly overbalanced.

'I mean, can you make people into film stars?' said William.

Mr Klein shrugged his padded shoulders.

'Make people into film stars?' he said. 'Listen, my child.'

And William listened. He had no chance of doing anything else. Mr Klein, having got an audience, however insignificant, evidently intended to make the most of it. One gathered that there was no film star of any magnitude on either side of the Atlantic who did not owe his or her position solely to Mr Adolph Klein. Waving his cigar so wildly that he nearly embedded it in William's eye, he went on to describe the debt owed to Adolph Klein by the French film, the Italian film, the Russian film . . . A feeling of panic came over William. For the first time in his life he had met his match in eloquence. But he raised his voice manfully to drown the sonorous notes of Mr Klein's recital.

'Yes, but listen,' he said. 'This girl I'm thinkin' of, she'd make a jolly good film star. She acts all right when she isn't gigglin' an' she went to the dentist las' week. We tried her on cats – I mean, changin' cats into wolf-hounds – but it got into a muddle.'

Adolph Klein was not listening. He was describing his last film. *Dusk at Morning*. It was simple, childlike, endearing, artistic, and at the same time staggering, stupendous, epoch-making, colossal. It held universal appeal. It had tears behind the laughter and laughter behind the tears. At this point he waved his walking-stick so violently that it caught in the hedge and he had to get down from his seat to retrieve it. William seized the opportunity to say:

'What's this film you're goin' to make next about?'

Strangely, the question penetrated Mr Klein's mind. Climbing back on to the stile, he launched into a lengthy description of his next film. It, too, was staggering and stupendous, simple and artistic. It had tears behind the laughter, laughter behind the tears. The highlight of the story was evidently the pursuit of the heroine by the villain across a railway bridge in which a thundering express train also played a part. The speed at which the girl ran outstripped both the villain and the express train. William sat up suddenly his eyes wide open.

'So this film star's got to be a good runner?' he said.

'Fleet as the wind,' said Mr Klein, waving his stick in circles round his head, 'and light as thistledown.'

'Well, now listen,' said William excitedly. 'If you saw a girl with eyelashes an' – an' special teeth an' – an' fleet as the wind, would you give her a job as a film star in this film?'

That started Mr Klein off again. He had genius, vision, a flair, hunches, what-have-you. He could spot a potential star at a glance, launch it in the twinkling of an eye. Given the right material, he could make stars out of nothing, out of nobody.

'Well, listen,' said William, his excitement now so great that he could hardly get the words out. 'This girl I'm thinkin' of, she'd make a star all right. She can run like a thistle an'—'

But Mr Klein had lost interest. For some time his eye had been roving round the countryside in search of a more worthy audience than this rapscallion of a small boy, and suddenly he espied a group of golfers entering the door of the Red Lion. Flinging away his half-smoked cigar and thrusting William aside with his stick, he crossed the stile, strode down the road to the Red Lion and entered its hospitable portals.

William picked himself up and ran off to find Ginger.

'I've got Ethel a job as a film star,' he said. ''Least, I've practic'ly got it. I've only got to see this man again and sort of fix things up. He doesn't mind 'em not bein' stars to start with. He's got visions an' hunches an' a lot more things I've forgot.'

Ginger was impressed but a little doubtful.

'Seems to me there's a good bit more fixin' up to be done,' he said.

'Oh, I'll manage that all right,' said William airily. 'I'll fix it up the nex' time I see him. I'm sure to be havin' another talk with him soon. He's jolly easy to talk to . . . I mean' – after a moment's thought – 'to listen to, an' he likes talkin' to me. I bet we'll be havin' another talk soon an' we'll fix it up then.'

But they didn't have another talk soon. Accosted by William on the road, Mr Klein waved him out of the way and strode on, deaf and blind to all the manoeuvres by which William tried to arrest his attention. He did not recognise William as the boy he had talked to on the stile. He never recognised his audiences. They were audiences and nothing else. Moreover, he had adopted a new pose. Adapting himself to his surroundings, he was no longer a film magnate. He was a country gentleman. He wore tweeds and talked about the harvest. He was learning the difference between a Saddleback and a Berkshire, between a Shorthorn and a Friesian.

The process had been started by the discovery that Sir Gerald and Lady Markham, the owners of Marleigh Manor, usually gave a Fête in the grounds during the summer, and Mr Klein decided that it was his duty as the tenant to carry on this tradition of Old English Country Life. He had, moreover, decided that it should outshine every other fête that had ever been held. It was to be a mixture of an Olde English May Day and a continental carnival, with a smattering of the Festival of Britain and a Hampstead Heath Bank Holiday. It was to be staggering and stupendous, simple and artistic, full of universal appeal.

He insisted on the word 'Revels' being printed on the posters in place of the word 'Fête'. He held meetings. He read up descriptions of Merrie England. He decided suddenly to have the whole thing filmed . . . then decided not to.

William assembled his Outlaws in the old barn.

'He won't listen to me talkin' now,' he said. 'He's busy over the Fête thing. I mean this Revels thing. An' I've *got* to get Ethel this job.'

'Oh, gosh!' groaned Douglas. 'I hoped you'd forgot that.'

''Course I've not,' said William. 'I got so jolly near it, talkin' to him, that I bet I can get it all fixed up with a bit more trouble. I've only to think out a plan, that's all.'

'I don't see what plan you can think out,' said Douglas. 'I should think after that cat business you'd leave it alone.'

''Course I can think out a plan,' said William. 'That cat business was ever so long ago. I've got well on with this film star plan since then.'

'You tried to get her a spy job,' Henry reminded him, 'an' it didn't come off.'

'Well, I might get her one yet,' said William. 'There's no tellin' what sort of job I'll get her, only jus' now I'm goin' on with this film star idea. He practic'ly promised it me an' then he sort of forgot.'

'Well, I don't see what you can do about it,' said Ginger.

'Well, I do,' said William. 'I've got a sort of idea comin' already. I've got to make her do somethin' at this Fête-Revel thing that'll show him she's a good film star. I can't tell her about it 'cause it'd put her straight off it. She's got a funny sort of idea that I muddle things up an' I can't get her out of it, but if I could sort of make her do somethin' – the sort of thing film stars do – without her knowin' it was me makin' her do it—'

'Gosh!' said Douglas. 'It's startin' gettin' complicated again. I knew it would.'

William was silent for a few moments, then a light broke out over his countenance.

'I've *got* it,' he said. 'This girl in this film he told me about had to run over a bridge an' there's a bridge in the garden of Marleigh Manor where this Fête-Revel thing's goin' to be. There's that lake with the island in the middle an' the bridge over to the island an' then right on from the island to the other side. If I could make her run over that bridge fleet as a thistle, same as he said, I bet he'd give her the job.'

'Yes, but how *can* you?' said Henry.

'That's what I've got to think out,' said William. 'I've got so jolly near it I'm not goin' to give up now.'

He returned home silent and thoughtful. His silence and thoughtfulness were not noticed by his family, whose attention was wholly absorbed by the coming 'Revels' at Marleigh Manor.

'I wish they were having races,' said Ethel. 'They always had races there at the Fêtes when I was a little girl and I always used to win them. I wish they hadn't gone out of fashion.'

'What sort of races were they?' said Jimmy Moore, who had dropped in for the evening.

'I liked the Obstacle Races best,' said Ethel. 'The sort they used to have there when we were children. They called them Secret Orders Obstacle races and they gave you a slip of paper with all the things you had to do on it. Everyone had a different one and you hadn't to tell anyone else what was on yours and there was someone to time them all. They put at the top of the paper where you'd got to start from and the time you'd got to start and someone blew a whistle and it was such fun . . . '

'I'll speak to the great man about it,' said Jimmy, 'and see if I can get him to revive it.'

William gave a gasp.

'What's the matter with you?' said Ethel.

William hastily assumed the blank expression by which he was wont to disarm suspicion.

'Nothin',' he said, then hurried round to Ginger's house and summoned him by the raucous yodel that was their usual signal.

'I say, Ginger,' he said breathlessly when Ginger joined him at the gate, 'I've got that idea. It's a jolly good one. Listen.'

Ginger listened, his eyes growing rounder and rounder.

'Sounds a bit difficult,' he said doubtfully at the end.

'All good ideas are a bit diff'cult,' said William airily. 'I bet it'll work out all right an' she'll be jolly grateful to me when she's got her photos in all the papers for tooth-paste an' things same as film stars do.'

'Well, how do we start?' said Ginger.

'Let's c'lect the others an' go an' see how that bridge is fixed up,' said William. 'We want to make it easy for her to run over like a thistle.'

They collected the others, made their way to Marleigh Manor and crawled through the hedge into the part of the grounds where the lake was. The lake was a gloomy stretch of water, overhung by trees, with an island in the middle connected with the mainland on either side by a ramshackle bridge. It was some distance from the rest of the garden and was screened off by a belt of trees. A tumbledown summer-house stood in a cluster of shrubs on the bank. The Outlaws had frequently used it in their games and the hole in the hedge that was their unauthorised entrance was worn into a fair-sized gap.

They found the entrance to the bridge blocked by a cord from which hung a half-obliterated notice, 'Danger.'

'We don't want to get her drowned,' said William, removing the cord and notice. 'Let's go'n' see what's wrong with it.'

The boards were a bit wobbly the las' time we played pirates on it. Come on. There's no one about.'

They made their way cautiously towards the middle of the bridge. Three of the boards were almost rotted away.

'We can't do it, then,' said Douglas with a sigh of relief.

William considered.

'She can swim all right if she falls in,' he said. 'It might be a good idea to let this film man see her swimmin' fleet as a thistle, too . . . but p'raps we'd better stick to this film about runnin' over a bridge . . . An' we've got to start by mendin' the boards so's she won't fall in.'

'I don't see how we can mend them,' said Ginger.

William had been considering the boards with frowning interest. Suddenly his brows cleared.

'*Tell* you what,' he said. 'There's that old packing-case in Douglas's garage. I bet the top of it's jus' about the same size as these three boards an' it's jolly strong wood. We could slip it in here 'stead of the three boards an' it'd make it safe as safe for her to run over. Let's take them out now an' Douglas can take them home an' see if this packing-case top's the same size.'

'This Fête thing's tomorrow,' said Henry. 'I mean, this Revels. We've got to fix it up pretty quick if we're goin' to fix it up at all.'

'All right,' said William. 'We'll fix it up quick. I'm jolly good at fixin' things up quick.'

The day of the Revels was fine and sunny. Mr Klein had dressed himself with much care as an English country gentleman in a pearl grey lounge suit and white waistcoat, with a carnation in his buttonhole – he had been dissuaded with some difficulty from appearing in a grey frock coat and top hat. A large crowd had gathered when Mrs Brown and Ethel arrived. Ethel, wandering off in search of her friends, was

urprised to find a piece of paper being thrust into her hand.
lenry had carried out his part of the plan well. There was no
ign of him when she looked round for the mysterious donor.
he read the paper and her eyes danced with amusement.
immy had said that the great man had refused to listen to him
hen he made the suggestion of the obstacle race, but evi-
ently he had pulled it off, after all. Henry had typed the
otice on his father's typewriter – on which he had had a good
eal of unofficial practice – looking out all the words in the
ictionary to make sure of the spelling. The result was, on the
hole, fairly creditable:

SECRET ORDERS OBSTACLE RACE
  Be behind bush behind summer-house opposite
bridge of lake at three o'clock. When whistle blows run
as quick as you can across bridge, round lake, jump gate
into paddock, run across paddock and round stables,
pick apple from orchard and return to bush.

'We've got to give her somethin' to do beside run across
le bridge,' William had said, 'or she wouldn't think it was a
al obstacle race. It doesn't matter what she does an' we
on't make it too obstacly or she won't bother with it.'
  William had assigned a definite part to each Outlaw. Henry
as to write the notice and deliver it to Ethel, Ginger was to
e posted halfway up a tree near the lake with his whistle,
Douglas was to have replaced the rotting boards by the pack-
lg-case lid before the Revels started and William was to lure
le film magnate to the lake at three o'clock. William's part
as the most difficult and not even William himself felt very
ptimistic about it, but to his surprise it turned out unexpect-
dly easy.
  After greeting his guests and playing the English country
entleman for about half an hour, Mr Klein suffered one of

his swift changes of mood. Quite suddenly he seemed t
sense the hollowness of the social whirl, the emptiness c
social gatherings, the dreariness of Revels. A convictio
swept over him that he was at heart a recluse, a solitary,
communer with Nature. Exchanging his genial smile for
heavy scowl, he withdrew from his guests and stood on th
outskirts of the group in an attitude of solitary contemplatio

It was at this moment that William approached him.

'Would you like to come and have a look at the lake, sir'
he said.

Anxiety had lent a sombre tinge to William's freckle
countenance. Mr Klein gazed at him with interest. He was n
conscious of ever having spoken to this boy before, but, chil
as he was, he was evidently a kindred spirit. Here was n
forced geniality, no jarring heartiness, no counterfeit affa
bility. This boy's face wore a look of fixed and settled gloor
that Mr Klein, in his present mood, found highly congenial.

'The lake?' said Mr Klein vaguely.

Faint memories came to him of a dreary stretch of wate
overhung by trees, a ramshackle bridge, a mouldering sum
mer-house. The scene fitted in so well with his mood that h
almost brightened.

'Yes . . . this way,' said William, leading his host awa
from the lawn, down a laurel-infested path to the dank lak
with its overhanging trees.

'There!' he said nervously. 'It's an int'restin' sort of bridg
isn't it? To watch, I mean. I sometimes feel I could stand ar
watch it for hours an' hours an' hours. I mean—'

He glanced at the stable clock, which could be seen ov
the trees. Three minutes to three . . . He had felt doubts of h
ability to engage Mr Klein in conversation for any length c
time, but he realised with relief that this would not be nece:
sary. Mr Klein did not need to be engaged in conversation. H
was discoursing with all his accustomed eloquence on th

eauty of solitude, the charm of seclusion, the lure of the ermit's life . . . but his eyes were straying in the direction of ie lawns and the sound of the band, and it was evident that is mood of aloofness was already on the wane.

'In a minute,' said William hoarsely, 'you're goin' to see ie mos' beautiful girl you've ever seen doin' jus' what you vant done in your new film. She'll come runnin' over that ridge fleet as a thistle an'—'

His mouth dropped open and his voice trailed away.

Something was happening, and it wasn't what he'd meant ɔ happen.

'he Outlaws had all fulfilled their allotted tasks except Jouglas, and Douglas had been dogged by characteristic ill-ɪck. At first everything had seemed to be going well. He had ɪken the three rotting boards home and found on measuring ɪem that the packing-case lid would exactly fill the gap they ɪad left. He intended to take it round early in the morning of ie Revels, but his mother had sent him on an errand into Iadley and he lost his return fare and had to walk back. He et off after lunch in good time, carrying his packing-case lid, ntered the side gate of the Manor – he had decided that the ɪd was too big for the hole in the hedge – and proceeded own the path that led to the lake. And there halfway down ie path—he met Miss Tufton. She advanced upon him, her ace wearing an expression of stern accusation.

'You're one of those naughty boys who set their dog on my ɪats,' she said severely.

'I'm s-s-sorry,' said Douglas, backing away before her.

'Are you aware,' she said, 'that as a result of your outrageous onduct one of my pussies is still in a highly neurotic state and ɪat another was so upset that she refused to touch her sardines ɪl the next day?' She continued to advance upon him and Jouglas continued to back before her, blinking nervously. 'Are

you aware that a hole several inches long was torn in my ne
curtains during the disgraceful affray and that the glass of
photograph of a beloved aunt was smashed to smithereens'
Her glance fell upon the packing-case lid. 'What is that an
where are you taking it? What mischief are you up to now? Te
me your parents' name and I will—'

Panic-stricken, Douglas had turned to flight. At first h
thought that his enemy was pursuing him and he dodge
behind a bush, intending to wait till she should have passec
then he saw that she had sat down on a garden seat on the pat
where he had met her and was idly surveying the landscape
He daren't pass her and he couldn't think of any other way c
reaching the lake. Douglas was a well-meaning boy, but h
had no initiative. Without William to tell him what to do, h
just didn't know what to do. Feeling as if he were in the gri
of a nightmare, he cowered behind his bush, clasping hi
packing-case lid, while the precious moments slipped by.

Ethel had been in two minds about the mysterious notice tha
had been slipped into her hand. At one moment she decided t
ignore it. At the next she decided to go through with it
Beneath her pose of sophistication there was a strong strea
of adventure and curiosity in Ethel's character, and she finall
decided at any rate to go to the bush at about three o'clock.

She took up her position between it and the summer-hous
to await developments . . . and suddenly, as she stood there
she heard low voices inside the summer-house. Two mer
were talking.

'Well, now, it's all fixed up, isn't it?' said one voice. 'The
safe's in the library and you've got the combination. All th
staff's out on the grounds, and you ought to have a clear field
Get the stuff as quick as you can, mix with the people on th
lawn a bit when you come out then make your way slowly int
the road. I'll be there with the car under the chestnut tree.'

ETHEL SAW TWO MEN COME OUT OF THE SUMMER-HOUSE.

Ethel peeped round her bush. Two men had come out of the summer-house. One of them, wearing a check overcoat, began to stroll in an apparently aimless fashion towards the house. The other, in a dilapidated raincoat, sloped off towards the entrance gate.

Ethel, despite her air of fragile beauty, was a girl of courage and resource. She set off at a run to the marquee where she had seen a policeman standing on guard over the prizes.

'Come to the house quick,' she panted. 'To the library. I'll explain as we go.'

The policeman wasted no time in questions and within a couple of minutes they had come on the man in the check overcoat, kneeling by the safe, slipping jewel-cases into his pocket.

The man in the check overcoat also wasted no time in questions.

He had explored the ground beforehand and had his retreat all ready in case of need. A couple of flying leaps over the bridge to the island, another couple on to the further bank, a plunge through the hole in the hedge – he had marked the Outlaws' private entrance – a dive into the car beneath the chestnut tree . . . and this bunch of rustics would be left far behind.

THE MAN IN THE CHECK OVERCOAT DROPPED THROUGH
THE HOLE INTO THE LAKE BELOW.

It was the figure of the man in the check overcoat that burst
upon the astonished gaze of William and Mr Klein, as they
stood watching the bridge. It took the first half of the bridge
in a series of running leaps then dropped clean through the
gaping hole into the lake below. The figure of the policeman
followed it, also dropping clean through the hole. The two
closed in the shallow water.

'Stupendous!' cried Mr Klein.

There was a wild surge of 'revellers' towards the lake. Above the general confusion could be heard the voice of William upraised indignantly.

'But it's all *wrong*! It isn't what we *meant*.'

The Outlaws were walking slowly down the road. They had stayed at the Revels till the mystery of the man in the check overcoat had been cleared up, had watched his ignominious departure in charge of the policeman, had spent what money they had on ice-creams and the hoop-la, and were now making their way homeward.

'Well, you didn't get that job for Ethel, after all,' said Henry.

William had been bewildered and dejected by the failure of his plan, but his bewilderment and dejection were vanishing. William could never be bewildered or dejected for long. His swagger was returning. He walked with his accustomed jauntiness.

'I said you wouldn't,' said Douglas.

'Well, that's where you're all wrong,' said William, ''cause I did get her a job.'

'You didn't.'

'I did. I got her the job I said I would all along.'

'Well, what job did you get her, then?'

'I got her a jolly good job as a spy.'

Chapter 8

William's Civil War

It was not often that William's stocky towsled figure did not head the crowd of boys who surged out of the big iron gate at the close of school, but today he was unusually slow, walking in a fashion that was almost meditative, his brow deeply furrowed, his lips compressed.

Ginger, Henry and Douglas were waiting for him in the road.

''Couldn't think what had happened to you,' said Ginger.

'I've been thinkin',' said William.

They looked at him for a moment in silence, impressed by the portentousness of his voice and expression.

'What about?' said Henry.

'About that hist'ry lesson,' said William.

'Gosh!' said Douglas, voicing the general amazement, for William did not as a rule waste much thought on the instruction that his schoolmasters so painstakingly imparted to him.

'Well, you see, I sort of got listenin' an' couldn't stop,' said William, a note of apology in his voice.

'I've forgot what it was about,' said Douglas.

'Wars of the Roses,' said Henry.

'That's a soppy name for it,' said William. 'I'd have made 'em call it somethin' diff'rent if I'd been there. Wars of the Supermen or Wars of the Tiger-Hearts, or somethin' like that. I'd have found somethin' better than' – in a tone of deep disgust – 'roses'.

'But what were you *thinkin'* about it?' said Ginger.

'Well, I was thinkin' it's time they came back. Civil wars, I mean. Can't think why they stopped havin' them. They're much better than all these abroad wars. Cheaper, too, 'cause you've not got to waste money on tickets goin' out abroad to 'em, an' you could come home to dinner when you wanted to. Why, it'd *save* money, havin' a civil war. An' there wouldn't be all this messin' about with foreign langwidges. Every-one'd understand what everyone else said. There's no *sense* in foreign langwidges, anyway. They had civil wars in hist'ry an' it's a pity they ever stopped.'

'There was one where a king hid in an oak tree an' his en-emies went underneath an' didn't see him,' said Henry, who could never resist airing his knowledge.

'Well, that was a jolly excitin' thing to happen,' said William. 'I bet that never happened in an abroad war. An' I bet when we start this civil war—'

'Gosh!' said Henry, taken aback. 'We can't start a civil war!'

The four were walking down the road, hands thrust deeply into pockets. William's face wore the look of illumination that one of his Ideas always brought to it, and the faces of the others wore the look of mingled interest and apprehension with which they were wont to receive William's Ideas.

'I don't see why not,' said William.

'You can't have a war with only four,' said Ginger.

'It'd be safer to stick to Cowboys an' Indians,' put in Douglas nervously.

'You can *start* with four,' said William. 'Wars spread . . . Well, p'raps we'd have to get a few more in, but I bet every-one'll want to join once they hear about it. They mus' be sick of abroad wars. I bet everyone'd be glad to have a civil war for a change.'

'Well, you've got to have somethin' to fight about,' said Henry. 'You can't jus' start fightin' about nothin'.'

'Oh, we'll soon find somethin' to fight about,' said William. 'What did they fight about in that one ole Frenchie was talkin' about this mornin'? I was thinkin' so much about havin' a new one that I kept forgettin' to listen to the old one.'

'Well,' said Henry after a moment's thought, 'one side was for the government an' the other side was against it.'

'That's not bad,' said William critically. 'I bet we can think up somethin' better than that, but it's not bad.'

'An' you can't have a war without an army,' objected Ginger.

'All right. I'll get an army,' said William. 'It's easy enough gettin' an army . . . Tell you what! I'll get two armies an' they can take sides an' fight against each other. That'll be a start anyway.'

'Yes, the start's all right,' said Douglas. 'It's the finish that gen'rally goes wrong.'

But the others, as usual, were becoming interested despite their first misgivings.

'It'll be jolly excitin' even if it doesn't spread,' said Ginger.

'Oh, it'll spread all right,' said William.

'When'll we start?' said Douglas, who was becoming infected by the others' enthusiasm.

'This afternoon,' said William. 'That's the best of a civil war. You can start it straight away without havin' to go out to foreign places to start it. We'll start it this afternoon.'

William's first step in the raising of an army was a notice fixed to the door of the old barn.

a sivil war will brake out this afternun at three oklock fre to ennyone bring weppons.
cined William Brown.

The response to the appeal was gratifying, and volunteers began to straggle into the old barn soon after half past two.

Fortunately Arabella Simpkin – who usually led the hecklers at William's meetings – was in bed with mumps and the audience listened to William's speech with comparative docility.

'Now listen, everyone,' he said. 'We're goin' to have a civil war 'stead of all these abroad ones. We won't have to pay to go abroad for it an' it'll save the gov'ment a lot of money an' they ought to be jolly grateful to us.'

A ragged cheer arose, followed by a babel of excited conversation.

'Well, go on listenin' to me,' said William, raising his voice above the uproar, ''cause I'm goin' to go on makin' this speech I'm makin'. We're goin' to have a civil war same as I said, an' it's a jolly good idea 'cause no one need know any foreign langwidges to fight it an' we can come home to dinner when there's anything we like same as trifle or jelly.'

'Or chocolate blancmange,' piped a small voice.

'I've seen a picture of abroad,' piped another small voice. 'There's crocodiles there.'

'Well, there's not much to crocodiles,' said William. 'There's crocodiles in the zoo if you want to see 'em. There jus' isn't any point in havin' them abroad as well. There's no sense in abroad at all . . . Anyway, we're goin' to start this civil war now an' we've got to get the armies goin' for it. You've all brought jolly good weapons.' He surveyed with approval the forest of broom handles, shovels, bows, arrows and air-guns that stretched in front of him. 'If we're bringing back civil wars we ought to bring back real fightin', too, same as heroes used to do in olden times, not jus' lettin' off bombs at each other without havin' a real bash at anyone. You'll find a civil war jolly excitin'. Henry knows about one where a king climbed an oak tree an' hid in it an' his enemies went underneath it an' it was jolly excitin'.'

'I bet I could climb an oak tree without havin' to go to war about it,' said a small boy with projecting teeth and a deep throaty voice.

'Oh, shut up!' said William. 'Now listen. We've got to be half on one side an' half on the other for a civil war. I'm goin' to be the gen'ral of one side an' the other side can be the en'my an' pick its own gen'ral. Hands up those who want to be on my side!'

Every hand went up.

'Now hands up those who want to be the en'my.'

There was no movement.

William, though gratified, was a little disconcerted.

'You've *got* to have an enemy for a war,' he said earnestly. 'You can't have a war with everyone on one side. Stands to reason . . . Now let's try again an' some of you must be the en'my. Now, hands up, the en'my!'

No hand rose.

'Oh, well,' said William with a shrug of resignation, 'we'll jus' have to be one army an' go out an' find an en'my . . . Come on.'

They straggled down the road behind him, singing, shouting, scuffling. The vanguard consisted of a pair of twins with upturned, inquiring noses and curly hair. One wore a bus conductor's outfit and the other was almost completely swallowed by an airman's cap and tunic.

Something of William's carefree zest began to desert him as the procession wended its way along the road.

'Gosh!' he said to Ginger. 'I never heard of anyone leadin' an army to battle with no one to lead it to battle against. I bet it's the first time it's ever happened in hist'ry.'

They were passing the gate of The Hall and suddenly William stopped. The grounds seemed to be full of young men in blazers standing about in groups, engaged in animated conversation, or sitting in deckchairs, writing in notebooks.

'Gosh!' said William. 'Is Mrs Bott havin' a party?'

'No, the Botts are away,' said Henry. 'They've let it.'

'They seem to've let it to a jolly big fam'ly,' said William.

'It can't be one fam'ly,' said Ginger, looking at the crowd of youths on the lawn. 'It mus' be dozens of fam'lies.'

'P'raps the garden's thrown open to the public,' said Henry knowledgeably. 'They do that sometimes.'

The army brandished its weapons restively and raised a tentative war cry.

'Jus' wait a minute,' said William, 'while I find out about it.'

The army subsided into an expectant silence and William approached two youths who were just emerging from the gate.

''Scuse me,' he said in a tone of elaborate politeness, 'but could you kin'ly tell me if it's a party or a fam'ly or jus' a garden thrown open at the public?'

One of the youths was tall and supercilious-looking. The other was shorter, with a pleasant friendly face.

'What business is it of yours?' said the taller one haughtily.

The other was looking with interest at the 'army' that straggled in William's rear.

'Who are these?' he said.

'You'll know all right,' said William darkly, 'when it spreads an' when we find an en'my an'——'

'Oh, come on,' said the tall youth impatiently.

'I'll tell you who we are and what we're doing here,' said the other. 'It's a Summer School for young Conservative workers. We're all young Conservative workers and we're having lectures and studying politics. *Now* are you satisfied?'

'Conservatives?' said William with sudden interest. 'You're all *for* the gov'ment then?'

'Most decidedly.'

'Oh, come on,' said the tall youth, adding, to William, 'and clear off with your circus and be quick about it!'

They set off down the road and William turned excitedly to address his army.

'Now listen, everyone,' he said. 'We've found the en'my.' Henry said that in the old civil war one side was for the gov'nment an' the other side was against it . . . Well, all these people that've taken the Botts' house are *for* the gov'ment so we'll be against it an' that'll make it a civil war same as the old one, so now we've got the en'my an' can have the war.'

'When can we start climbin' oak trees?' said the deep throaty voice.

'Oh, shut up about oak trees,' said William. 'We've got to start this war first.'

He peeped through the hedge and looked at the figures dotted about the lawn. They were large, athletic, muscular. Regarded in the light of an enemy, they seemed to take on a more formidable air.

'They look jolly *strong*,' said Douglas.

'Yes, but we'll attack 'em off their guard,' said William.

'There's a nice little tree over there,' said the deep throaty voice. 'I'd rather climb that than an oak tree.'

'Well, we're not *goin'* to climb trees,' said William. 'We're goin' to attack the en'my an' conquer it.'

'Well, let's get started,' said Ginger.

'Y-yes,' said William slowly. 'Yes, we'd better get started.' Again he peered through the hedge at the muscular athletic forms. 'P'raps we'd better not attack 'em straight off from here. They'd see us comin' across the grass an' they might overpower us . . . Tell you what! We'll go round to the other side an' we'll creep round the house an' they won't see us comin' an' we can attack 'em suddenly an' take 'em off their guard.'

'I don't think there's enough trees for all of us,' said the deep throaty voice. 'Bags me that little one, anyway.'

'Oh, shut up about trees,' said William. 'Now are you ready? Quick March!'

The army set off at a good pace, making its way in high

spirits and ragged formation along the field path that bordered the hedge till it reached the back of the estate.

'Yes, this is all right,' said William. 'Now we'll creep quietly through the hedge into the garden an' then creep quietly round the house an' attack 'em.'

They made their way through the hedge, jostling and pushing each other, getting their weapons entangled, engaging in miniature battles as they charged through the thick growth.

'Now we'll creep across this bit of garden,' said William. 'There's lots of bushes we can creep round . . . Here! Come out of there!'

For the vanguard of the army had straggled into a greenhouse that stood near the gate. It emerged, smiling apologetically.

'There was a little chimney goin' up through the roof,' it explained, 'an' we wanted to find out how it worked. We did find out. 'Least, I think we did . . . '

'Well, you've come here to fight a civil war,' said William sternly, 'not to find out how chimneys work. Now listen an' I'll tell you again. We'll creep across this bit of garden, then creep round the house an' then attack all of a sudden 'cause no one'll see us comin'.'

But he was wrong. Someone did see them coming. They had not noticed a small gnome-like gardener who was watering a bed of Zinnias with a garden hose behind a clump of bushes. He swung round at the sound of the advancing army and stared at it in incredulous amazement – an amazement that gradually gave place to fury. Boys were his pet aversion, and here they were, ranks upon ranks of them, invading his garden with the outrageous impudence of their kind. Unhesitatingly he turned the hosepipe on them.

Winded by the sudden attack, dripping with water, the army turned to flee – all except William and Ginger, who took refuge behind a holly bush, realising too late that their retreat

THE GARDENER TURNED THE
HOSEPIPE ON THEM.

was cut off and that the gardener was advancing on them with his hosepipe.

'Come on,' said William. 'It's time to start that tree-climbin'. Here's a tree. Gosh! It's an oak tree, too. Come on quick or we'll be too late.'

But the gardener, abandoning his hosepipe, came scuttling across the lawn and grabbed them as they were still trying to find a foothold on the trunk.

'Hi! You leave us alone,' said William. 'We've got an army. We—'

'Little varmints,' muttered the gardener as he pulled them down. 'Blasted little varmints . . . I'll learn ye, I will.'

He dragged them, protesting loudly, to a shed near the greenhouse, opened the door, flung them in, closed the door and turned the key in the lock.

'Ye can stay there,' he said. 'Ye can stay there till you've learned yourselves manners. Trespassin' an' destroyin' of property! Blasted little varmints! . . . As if I'd not got enough on me hands with all that pottin' to do in the greenhouse without . . . '

His voice died away in angry mutterings.

'Well, it wasn't much of a civil war,' said Ginger bitterly as he picked himself up from a heap of fertiliser.

'It's not finished yet,' said William doggedly.

He had been less fortunate than Ginger. Evidently the shed contained the oddments of dressings that the gardener applied to his soil. Ginger had fallen on a pile of fertiliser, but William had landed on a pile of soot salvaged from some recent chimney-cleaning operations. The soot adhered readily to his dripping person, and Ginger gave a gasp of horror as he arose.

'Gosh!' he said. 'You do look awful. You're all black.'

'Well, I bet you're almost as bad,' said William. 'You're all white . . . Anyway, I don't care what I look like. I'm jolly well goin' to finish this war. We've lost the first battle, but that's nothin'. Lots of people in hist'ry lost the first battle an' won the war in the end. Axshully it's a good thing to lose the first battle, 'cause it puts the en'my off their guard an' makes 'em easier to conquer.'

'But you've not got an army,' said Ginger.

'I can manage all right without an army,' said William. 'Axshully an army's a bit of a nuisance an' I'm glad Henry an' Douglas took it away. The first thing we've got to do is get out of this shed. I bet—'

He stopped. People were passing the shed in little groups on their way to the house, using the back entrance, evidently, because it was nearer the village. Peering through the dust-encrusted window, he recognised well-known local figures – Miss Milton, General Moult, Mrs Monks . . . Snatches of conversation reached him.

'It should be a most interesting afternoon. He's an excellent speaker, I believe.'

'Yes. So kind of them to ask the local people.'

'Well, it's all political propaganda, I suppose. Having a

cabinet minister down to speak is a wonderful draw, of course.'

'Asking us to tea, too. So kind!'

'Oh, yes. All the trimmings.'

'Gosh!' said William. 'There mus' be a sort of meetin' up at the house an' they're all goin' to it.'

'Let's get away as quick as we can,' said Ginger. 'We can't fight all those p'litical people an' anyway they'll all be inside the house listenin' to the speech.'

'Well, they aren't the en'my now,' said William grimly. 'That ole gardener's the en'my now. It's a civil war between me an' that ole gardener now. If he thinks he can soak me with water an' then push me into soot, he's jolly well mistaken.'

'No, he isn't,' Ginger pointed out, ''cause he has done.'

'Well, he's goin' to get somethin' back,' said William. 'He's won the first battle but he's jolly well goin' to lose the last one. We'll wait till we're quite sure they're all in the house listenin' to the speech an' then we'll go on with this civil war.'

There came the sound of distant clapping from the house.

'There!' said William. 'They're all in the house listenin' to the speech now . . . I bet this window opens. There's a sort of latch under all this dirt an' cobwebs . . . Yes, here it is . . . It's all rusted up, but—'

With an effort he pulled up the rusty latch and forced the small window open.

'Yes, we can get out now,' he said, 'an' start the war prop'ly.'

'But what are you goin' to *do*?' said Ginger as they climbed with some difficulty through the narrow aperture. William jumped to the ground and looked about him.

The garden appeared to be empty. The hosepipe lay unattended along the grass.

'I'm goin' to soak *him* with water same as he did me, then

I'll have won the last battle an' winnin' the last battle means winnin' the war.'

'You don't know where he is,' said Ginger.

'Yes, I do. He said he'd got to do pottin' in the greenhouse so he'll be in the greenhouse.'

They turned to look at the greenhouse. It appeared to be full of swirling black smoke.

'Gosh! What's that!' said Ginger.

'I bet he's smokin' some awful tobacco,' said William. 'He *would* smoke awful tobacco . . . Look! There's a window open in the roof. I bet I can get the water in at him through that. Come on. Let's start.' Another burst of clapping came from the house. 'They're all settled inside there. No one can stop us.'

'S'pose someone comes late an' catches us at it,' said Ginger.

William considered.

'Well, if they do, I'm goin' back to foreign wars,' he said. 'If you can't speak English they can't do anythin' to you . . . Come on. You go an' turn on the tap an' I'll send the water on him through the window. Are you ready? One, two, three . . . *Go!*'

Ginger turned on the tap and William directed the stream of water through the open skylight window. So intent was he on his task that he did not notice an erect old gentleman in formal morning suit coming down the path till a hand descended on his shoulder and a voice said,

'What are you doing there, my boy?'

William looked up at his captor then bared his teeth in an ingratiating smile.

'Me no spick English,' he said.

Ginger had thrown in his hand, turning off the water at the tap and vanishing discreetly through the hedge.

Still holding William by the collar, the old gentleman

approached the greenhouse and, opening the door, peered into its murky depth. To William's surprise and annoyance there was no sign of the gardener.

'There seems to have been a little trouble here,' said the old gentleman. 'I think you've dealt with it quite efficiently. We'll leave the door open . . . '

William stared at him, murmuring again, 'Me no spick English.'

The old gentleman had now turned his attention to William, and was looking at him in a mystified fashion. William's ingratiating smile had shown white teeth in a dusky face. His immersion in the soot had been a thorough one. To a short-sighted observer – and the old gentleman was a very short-sighted one – the hue of his features was strongly suggestive of Eastern extraction.

'Perhaps you – er – live here or are staying here?' he said in a tone of kindly bewilderment.

'Me no spick English,' said William, casting an eye round for escape and finding none.

A maid crossed the lawn in the direction of the kitchen garden.

'Excuse me,' said the old gentleman courteously. 'Can you tell me anything about this little chap? Does he live here or – is he staying here?'

The maid glanced distastefully at William.

'Never seed 'im before,' she said, 'an' don't care if I never sees 'im again.'

'Oh dear!' said the old gentleman. 'He may have – strayed from somewhere. He appears to speak no English. Perhaps there's some sort of International gathering of foreign children in the neighbourhood?'

'There's somethink over at Marleigh,' she said. 'Scouts an' whatnot. There are some furrin' boys there.'

'Ah, yes!' said the old gentleman, vaguely. 'We are all brothers and sisters, my child.'

'Speak for yourself,' said the maid tartly. Her glance travelled again to William. 'I wouldn't 'ave '*im* for a brother, not fer nothin'.'

Then she went on her way with another toss of her head.

'Tut! Tut!' said the old gentleman sadly. 'What a long way we are still from the brotherhood of man!' He sighed. 'A good thing you didn't understand, my poor little fellow.'

'No, I didn't understand,' William assured him. 'Me spick no English.'

The old gentleman was not listening. He was looking in a worried fashion at the house, from which another burst of clapping had just come.

'Well, well . . . I'm shockingly late already. I'm afraid I mustn't waste any more time, but I don't like to leave you here without making further inquiries in case you really are lost, especially after your very helpful effort in the matter of the greenhouse. I should like to hand you over to your rightful guardians before I join our political friends. Or perhaps' – he brightened – 'Yes, perhaps that would be the best thing to do. Come along with me, my little man.'

William, who had now surrendered to Fate, let himself be led round the side of the house and in at the open french window. There was an improvised platform at one end of the room and the floor was filled by rows of seats occupied by a large and enthusiastic audience. A cheer greeted the old gentleman's entrance and the speaker stopped speaking and came to the edge of the platform.

'So glad you could come, Sir Claud. Come up on to the platform.'

Sir Claud went up on to the platform, still leading William. An ashen hue had invaded William's countenance beneath its covering of soot, but he bared his teeth again in a fixed and glassy smile and repeated doggedly, 'Me no spick English.'

'May I interrupt the meeting for one moment,' said Sir

'DOES ANYONE KNOW ANYTHING ABOUT THIS LITTLE
LAD?' ASKED SIR CLAUD.

Claud, 'to ask if any of you know anything about this little
lad? I'm told that there is some sort of International Youth
Gathering in the neighbourhood from which he may have
wandered. He speaks no English—'

'Me no spick English,' corroborated William hoarsely. His gaze went round the room and the fixed and glassy smile dropped from his lips as his eyes fell on his parents sitting in the second row, their faces slowly freezing into masks of horror.

'He evidently came into the grounds because he noticed from the road that something had gone wrong with the heating apparatus in the greenhouse' continued Sir Claud, 'and that the fumes, instead of going out through the 'flue pipe, were pouring into the greenhouse itself and doubtless harming the plants. He noticed also that the open skylight was just above the stove and, with an initiative and resource that

should be a model to our English boys, he took the hosepipe and sent the stream through the skylight directly upon the stove. A most ingenious and creditable action. The place was so full of smoke that he would have found difficulty in directing the stream through the door. I should like to tender our thanks to the little fellow and then restore him to his guardians who may be suffering anxiety on his account. We are, after all, in the place of hosts to these young foreigners and, as he speaks no English—'

'Me no spick—' began William again desperately. Then the words died away as, with set grim face, Mr Brown arose to claim his son.